Dear Romance Readers,

Finally, just in time for those long and lovely summer afternoons, your romance wishes have all come true. The BOUQUET line launches with four stories that will leave you begging for more—and four more will be coming your way every month!

We're celebrating the Bouquet debut with a delicious story by award-winning romantic favorite Leigh Greenwood. Leigh is a thoroughbred racing fan, and **The Winner's Circle** features a Kentucky bluegrass horse farm . . . and a sizzling love story. The heroine of Patricia Werner's **Sweet Tempest** is a meteorologist who flies into the eyes of hurricanes to collect data, but finds the stormiest passion in the arms of a charismatic storm chaser.

We wouldn't dream of launching a new line of romance without a story about a baby, and Kathryn Attalla, well known to Silhouette® and Precious Gems readers, has crafted a fetching one to grace the Bouquet debut lineup. Heroine Caitlin is forced to strike a hard bargain to hold onto her baby . . . (but can she hold onto her heart?) in **The Baby Bargain.** And we welcome newcomer Karen Drogin to the Bouquet list with **Perfect Partners**—two lawyers, first adversaries, then lovers, who learn that partnership means much more than billable hours.

Treat yourself to the bouquets that never wilt—sparkling romances you'll want to treasure on your keeper shelf. The kind of romance novels you read, then sigh and say, "Finally. Exactly the kind of book I really love."

The Editors

DEAL?

After the kiss, Griff pulled back slowly. Chelsie ran a trembling hand through her hair, a movement he stilled by lacing his fingers through hers. He cleared his throat, wondering how to broach the delicate subject after the intimacy they'd just shared. "We need to talk," he said.

The corners of her mouth turned up in a smile. "I think we just expressed ourselves quite clearly without words," she said.

"This isn't about that," he said. "I'm proposing a partnership. In law."

"What if we don't get along?"

Griff glanced down at their hands, still intertwined. His thumb traced circles on her soft skin. He reached out and brushed a strand of hair off her cheek.

"Do you make it a practice," Chelsie went on, "to mix business with pleasure?"

He chuckled. "No, but I am glad to know you'd label that kiss pleasure." He got serious. "You've got the experience dealing face-to-face with clients. My experience is with institutional clients. I could learn from you."

Chelsie tried to suppress a grin. "Cut the humble act," she said. "From what I've heard around family court, you talk circles around the most seasoned pros." She paused. "Okay," she whispered.

"You won't be sorry," he said.

"That, counselor, remains to be seen," Chelsie said. She grasped his outstretched hand. As her satiny skin brushed his calloused fingers, more than a business handshake passed between them. . . .

PERFECT PARTNERS

KAREN DROGIN

ZEBRA BOOKS
Kensington Publishing Corp.
http://www.zebrabooks.com

ZEBRA BOOKS are published by

Kensington Publishing Corp.
850 Third Avenue
New York, NY 10022

First Printing: July, 1999
10 9 8 7 6 5 4 3 2 1

Printed in the United States of America

To *the* perfect partner, my husband, Phillip, and to my special girls, Jaclyn and Jennifer.

A special thanks to Hudson Valley RWA for accepting me and helping me achieve my dream. And to Kathy, Renee, Janet, Bette, Claire, Terri, Eileen and Shannon . . . May all *your* dreams come true.

ONE

"I've reached a decision. Will the parties please rise?"

Chelsie Russell eased back her chair and rose to her feet, scrutinizing the white-haired judge who held her niece's fate in his hands. She didn't dare look at her mother and father seated to her left. She could barely face their lies and manipulations. For the first time in her life, Chelsie wanted to lose a case.

Representing her parents had been a foolish undertaking made under stressful, grief-filled circumstances. The untimely loss of her sister had been raw, the guilt for things not done acute. Having grown up in their home, she should have known her mother and father weren't cut out to be role models to a young child.

The judge cleared his throat. "Rendering a decision between family is never easy." He turned towards Griffin Stuart, a man Chelsie had wronged in ways she'd never intended. "You lost a brother in that car accident," the judge said.

Griffin nodded. Chelsie swallowed over the lump in her throat. With his dark hair and strong features, the resemblance to her niece was unmistakable. So was his devotion. His earlier testimony proved his suffering ran deep. She clutched the edges of the scarred wooden table.

The judge turned towards Chelsie's parents. "And you lost a daughter," he said with compassion. "Your desire to raise your granddaughter is understandable. Admirable even, but not at someone else's expense."

Chelsie agreed. She hadn't known her parents would breach the boundaries of fairness to obtain what they wanted. She only wished she had known. They all would have been spared this ordeal.

The judge continued. "No one benefits by lying and deceit. Nor will it gain you the result you seek. As a result, I hereby award full and permanent custody to the child's uncle, Griffin Stuart, with liberal visitation rights granted to the Russells, who I hope have learned from this experience." He banged his gavel. "Court is adjourned."

It was over. Chelsie laid her head in her hands as her parents stormed out of the room without a word.

Alone in the hallway, Chelsie leaned against the marble pillar and closed her eyes. Through her light silk blouse, the cold stone chilled her back and she shivered. Despite her relief over the outcome, common decency and her feelings for Griffin Stuart mandated she attempt to make amends.

She wondered if he'd even listen. Having avoided family functions, Chelsie's dealings with Griffin had been limited to professional affairs. They would pass one another at bar-related functions with a friendly nod and an occasional exchange of pleasantries. At times, she even thought she'd been the recipient of a lingering look, but knew she had to be mistaken. Or perhaps she'd just wanted to be. Though she'd given him an admiring glance of her own, her chosen lifestyle left no room for any man, especially one whose ties to her family drew her into an emotional minefield.

And now? They'd have to be civil for Alix's sake. Thanks to the judge's ruling, Griff couldn't deny her or her parents visitation, but she no longer expected him to greet her with an easy smile or a casual laugh. His reputation labeled him as a formidable attorney with a quick temper which he'd probably turn her way, given half a chance.

"Tough morning?"

Chelsie recognized that deep voice. Apparently, the endless day wasn't over yet. "More than you can imagine," she said as she lifted her gaze.

Hazel eyes blazed with unspoken anger and his blatant disgust charged the air around him. She remembered a time when those eyes had gazed upon her with friendly warmth. Looking at him now, aloof, distant, and treating her with disdain, she regretted the change. But she met the challenge without blinking.

She understood Griffin's contempt and wouldn't begrudge him his pain. She'd lost a sister. He'd barely gotten over the shock of losing his brother when she'd served him with custody papers.

She'd nearly cost him his niece, the only family he had left, and Chelsie knew that pain firsthand. She was intimately familiar with losing someone precious. "I just . . ."

"Don't tell me. It's always difficult to lose a case," he said with undisguised hostility.

She shook her head. "Not this time."

"Really?"

"Really. I owe you an apology."

"Save the *I'm sorrys* for someone who cares. You did your job and you lost. Just be thankful you did, or who knows what kind of life my niece would have had?"

"She's my niece, too."

"A lot of good that almost did her."

She winced because he was right. Because her parents had lost their daughter, Chelsie had succumbed to her mother's tears and her father's pleas, believing the couple would put their granddaughter first, before their active social life and status in the community. An orphaned little girl deserved more stability than one parent or guardian could offer. Chelsie had forgone fighting for custody herself because her single-parent home wasn't the best choice for her niece, nor was Griffin's. At least her parents could afford to care for the little girl, and Chelsie had planned on her own influence to compensate for her parents' shortcomings.

Lying, cheating, and attempted bribery. They'd gone overboard this time. She shivered in disgust. Given the choice between the carefree bachelor and her materialistic parents, she'd gambled on hope and her parents . . . and lost.

She shifted her attention to the man to whom she owed more than an apology. "You have every right to be angry, but I'm glad you won." Chelsie placed a hand on his arm. Searing heat and an unexpected jolt of awareness penetrated her fingertips. Warmth suffused her, awakening long dormant feelings. She shook her head, amazed a mere touch could ignite a flame so strong it threatened to consume her.

Though she forced her hand to remain on his muscled forearm, his heated strength settled inside her and shattered what little composure remained. "I'm sure you'll make a great father," she said, her words sounding hoarse to her ears.

"Uncle. She had a father."

She knew that without his curt reminder. Though she and her sister had drifted apart over the years, Chelsie still felt the loss. Griffin and his brother had been each other's only family. She couldn't begin to imagine his pain.

The last few weeks had shown her that he and Alix were as close as parent and child. He'd obviously spent more time with the little girl than Chelsie ever had. At one time, she believed she'd had good reason to back away. She couldn't be that selfish again.

Without warning, he jerked his arm back as if her touch repelled him. She curled her empty fingers into a fist.

Obviously, she'd been the only one to feel a powerful connection. She wouldn't allow him to know he'd shaken her. "Look, I'm sure raising a child won't be easy," she began.

"I can handle it." He folded his arms across his chest.

Her eyes followed the movement. He'd removed his suit jacket earlier. His paisley tie hung loose around his neck, and the first few buttons on his starched white shirt had been opened, revealing deeply bronzed skin.

He cleared his throat. She glanced up to find his intense eyes focused on hers. His gaze traveled the length of her body before finally settling once again on her now flushed face. But the effect of his heated gaze remained, evidenced by the tingling of her skin and the heaviness in her breasts. An appreciative glint sparkled in the depths of his dark eyes.

She had little time to ponder his reaction or her own surprising feelings. An instant later, the steely anger returned.

"Alix and I will be fine," he said in an abrupt voice, reminding her of all that lay between them.

Chelsie swallowed hard. "I didn't mean to imply otherwise. I just wanted to offer . . . I mean, if you should need help or anything . . ." She faltered.

"We won't." The chill in the air had nothing to do with the air conditioning. His cold stare told her in no uncertain terms that anything that passed between them had been one sided or existed only in her imagination.

Her overture had not been welcome. She sighed and thought of her niece. Though she had hoped to change his mind, she merely nodded her understanding.

"Look who Uncle Ryan has here." A deep voice interrupted them.

Grateful for the temporary reprieve, she shifted her gaze. Alix bobbed up and down on the shoulders of a dark-haired man who had occasionally sat behind Griffin in the courtroom, a man who seemed as close to Griffin and Alix as any family member.

Griffin reached over, lifted his niece from Ryan's arms, and held her close. Without warning, he tossed the two year old high, repeating the tickling episode Chelsie had seen many times that morning. The happy shrieks warmed her as nothing else could. At least her niece would have a happy life.

Seeing the smile on his face, Chelsie realized Griffin was a devastatingly handsome man. Coupled with his ability to put aside his grief for the sake of a child, Chelsie had learned much about him. She softened towards him once again.

Settled in her uncle's arms, Alix reached out a hand and touched Chelsie's hair. "Pretty."

"So are you," Chelsie said, ruffling the child's dark curls with her fingers.

"Mommy."

At the little girl's heartfelt plea, pain seared Chelsie's heart and she withdrew her hand. In truth, she had lost her sister long ago. Because Shannon's family had represented the kind of life Chelsie wanted but would always be denied, she'd made the difficult decision to pull back from the closeness the sisters had always shared.

Chelsie had suffered through an abusive marriage for too long, a mistake that had robbed her of the ability to have children, a family. A future. Wanting her younger sister to have all she couldn't, she had watched from the sidelines, assuring herself that Shannon's marriage wouldn't sour as her own had. That her sister remained happy and loved.

After a while, Chelsie had stayed away, remaining connected to her sister only by phone. Death had made the rift permanent.

"Want Mommy," Alix said, holding her hands out towards Chelsie.

"No, sweety, I'm not Mommy." She ignored the memories the statement brought and forcefully pushed aside the unwelcome reminders of what would never be.

"Hold me." The little girl threw her body forward. Griffin had no choice but to release her, Chelsie no choice but to take the child into her arms and hold her close.

Ignoring his grim expression, Chelsie planted a kiss on Alix's forehead. The sweet aroma of baby shampoo tickled Chelsie's nose, reminding her of why she'd always tried to keep a safe distance from this adorable child. In Alix, Chelsie saw too clearly the baby she'd lost and the children she'd never have. She closed her eyes and inhaled, savoring the unfamiliar yet comforting smell.

"Mommy," the child said, looking around.

Chelsie swallowed, forcing back the pain that lurked behind the unwelcome tears. "No, honey," she said again in a husky voice.

Griffin exhaled a sigh and reached for Alix.

Reluctantly, Chelsie handed the little girl back to her uncle. As she returned Alix to Griffin, the empty feeling in the pit of her stomach proved she'd been right. Any connection to this little girl would come at great emotional cost. Thanks to the jarring shift in family dynamics and the painful loss of her sister, Chelsie had no choice.

Obviously, Alix needed a connection to her mother. That was the least Chelsie could offer her sister's child. The little girl needed her, and she would reach out to Alix regardless of the emotional risk.

She met Griffin's gaze and was startled to find his eyes trained on her face.

"I guess you look more like Shannon than I realized," he said finally, shifting Alix in his arms. "She asks for Mommy and Daddy constantly." As he spoke, he took two steps back. He obviously begrudged her even a simple explanation.

Chelsie bit back a sigh. As a lawyer, she should be used to uphill battles, but he seemed determined to hold more than a grudge. Despite her reservations, she'd like more time with her niece in the future. The judge's ruling had assured her of that, but she realized now wasn't the time to ask.

"It'll get easier." She cringed as the platitude escaped her lips.

He remained silent. The other man stood to one side and watched them with obvious interest. Chelsie felt the heat of his gaze and looked over. He smiled and pulled his hand from the pocket of his jeans. "Ryan Jackson."

She grasped his hand, grateful for a friendly face in the enemy camp. "Chelsie Russell. Nice to meet you."

At the exchange of pleasantries, Griffin's gaze settled on their intertwined fingers and his expression darkened.

She picked up her briefcase. "As I said, I'm sorry. If there's anything I can do . . ."

"There's not." He didn't bother to couch his anger with niceties.

She sympathized with his pain, but did not have to take his abuse. "Right." She reached out to Alix, fingering her soft curls between her fingers.

Without another word, she turned and walked out of the building, away from the man and the child.

Griff scowled at Chelsie's retreating back, his gaze unwillingly fixed on the gentle sway of her hips as she walked. He grunted in disgust. There was nothing gentle about Chelsie Russell. He placed Alix beside him on the floor.

That he'd almost allowed himself to be distracted by Chelsie's dark eyes and huskily spoken words disgusted him. He couldn't let himself forget her attempt to separate him from his niece, a little girl she'd never given a second thought to until now.

Chelsie had never been one for family visits, and though he'd have liked to get to know her better, he hadn't been given the chance. He'd always admired her looks, and as an attorney, he'd respected her dedication and zeal, but he'd never expected her to turn those killer instincts on him.

Thanks to her misplaced family loyalty, he'd almost lost his niece, his last link to his brother. For that, he'd never forgive her.

"Cool off, buddy. You won. Alix is safe and she's yours."

"Yeah. Thanks for the surveillance tape, by the way." Proof that Chelsie's parents had attempted to bribe Griff into relinquishing custody had undermined every seemingly credible witness on their behalf and undoubtedly swayed the judge.

"What's a good P.I. for?"

Griff turned to watch Alix run in circles around the marble pillar. She looked so much like Jared that a lump formed in his throat. Once it lodged there, the accompanying emotional pain and memories would take time to subside.

The car accident that claimed the lives of his brother and sister-in-law had shaken the foundation of his existence. He and Alix had each other and no one else. The Russells didn't count, and for all the time she'd spent with the little girl, neither did Chelsie.

At two years old, Alix needed Griff to keep the memory of both parents alive in her heart and her mind. He would do that, even if he had to alter his entire lifestyle to accomplish it.

"Why do you suppose she takes on all those tough cases?" Ryan asked. He pulled a carrot from a paper bag and placed it in Alix's hand. "More than half of them are *pro bono*, you know."

"This doesn't count as one of her tough cases," Griff muttered. "And her parents don't exactly classify as those in need of free legal counsel. How do you know all this, anyway?"

"Had to do something with my time while I kept Alix away from the theatrics in there." He gestured towards the courtroom.

"Who the hell knows why women do what they do? Most of them want something." Griff could understand Chelsie's need to support family. He'd stuck by his brother all their lives. But a bright woman with an ounce of compassion would want more for her niece than to be raised by people capable of deceit and bribery. Even if they were her parents.

"Chelsie Russell's not Deidre."

Griff lifted one eyebrow. "No? Could have fooled me. She does a damned good imitation. She's out to build a reputation and doesn't care who she steps on in the process." His gaze drifted towards the glass doors Chelsie had disappeared through minutes before. "Trust me, Ryan. She'll get what she wants. I know the type."

"Maybe she's building that reputation, but seems

to me it's the other way around. Unlike some women, she gives. Doesn't take."

"Sure she does. You're just a sucker for a pretty face."

"Still bitter, huh? I guess it hasn't been that long, but I'd say you're better off without the witch."

"Drop it, Jackson." His fiancée hadn't had the decency to wait until Griff had buried his brother before she dumped him, his new charge, and a lifestyle that didn't fit into her plans. She'd turned out to be no better than the mother who had abandoned him as a child. Without a six-figure salary, Griff held little appeal. Deidre had stuck around only as long as he remained a partner at the largest firm in the city of Boston.

"What's all this hostility about anyway? The lady was just doing her job," Ryan said.

"A job that no self-respecting attorney would have taken. But hey, representing her parents must have garnered her some pretty wealthy clients."

Who cared if her own niece suffered in the process? Not Chelsie Russell. She'd proven her priorities. Morals and ethics weren't among them. He didn't ask himself why he cared so damned much that she'd disappointed him.

"The old folks did a number on her, couldn't you see that? Besides, somebody had to take their case. Everyone is entitled to legal representation. Isn't that the first thing they teach you in law school?"

Griff mumbled an expletive and caught Alix by the back of her shirt. "Hold it, squirt." The child stilled for all of two seconds before she took off to circle the pillar again. At least she'd stopped long enough to hand him the carrot and put two orange hand prints on his white shirt.

"Tell me something," Ryan said, in his I-know-something-even-you-don't tone of voice. "What's really bothering you? The fact that the Russells dragged you through a dirty court battle or that the lovely Miss Russell played opposing counsel?"

Griff cocked an eyebrow at Ryan. "What the hell do you think? I just spent the day fighting for custody of my brother's child," he said in a hushed yet angry voice. His niece was young, but bright. Griff didn't want her to remember any more of this awful day than was necessary. "I'd be furious no matter who tried to take Alix away from me."

"Right."

"Chelsie has nothing to do with this," Griff said in response to Ryan's disbelieving stare.

Then why did thoughts of dark eyes and soft-looking skin remain embedded in his mind? And why did her heated touch course through his clothing to reach somewhere inside him he'd closed off long ago?

Ryan shrugged. "You're the boss. If you're sure you're not interested, I just might be."

Griff grunted in disgust. "I'd bet she's not the dirty jeans and sneakers type."

"Low blow for someone who isn't interested."

"Shut up and let's get out of here."

"Mommy," Alix said.

Griff shook his head.

"Mommy," she wailed.

"Oh, hell," Griff mumbled as he took her little hand and walked to the door.

* * *

Griff popped the trunk of the family-style sedan and collected as many grocery bags as he could carry. After three trips to the house and back, he'd unloaded most of the packages. He marveled at the amount of food and other items necessary to care for a two year old. Since his niece had become a permanent part of his life, his purchases had expanded immensely. Diapers were but one new addition.

After lifting the last bag, he slammed the trunk closed. Alix's appetite amazed him. So did the fact that he'd traded in his beloved convertible for what the salesman had termed "the ultimate family car." Griff had nearly choked on the word *family*. That was before the man had slapped him on the back and cracked, "Must have been one hell of an argument. This baby's a lot more expensive than flowers or candy."

Griff grimaced at the memory. His sports car hadn't netted much as a trade-in. The guy was a crook, taking Griff's convertible for much less than what he'd paid. Still, he had to admit the man's views on women were sound. At this moment, Griff didn't have a hell of a lot of respect for the gender. He and Alix were a family. There wasn't a chance the twosome would turn into three.

He left the packages on the kitchen counter and went to trade places with Mrs. Baxter. After a day with an active two year old, the older woman probably needed a rest, unless the past few weeks of sleepless nights had finally caught up with Alix and she'd taken a nap. The poor little girl could use the sleep.

So, for that matter, could he. He was physically exhausted and emotionally drained. His life as a bachelor had left him ill-equipped to handle his niece and her night terrors, or whatever demons prevented the child from sleeping soundly.

The sliding glass door in the kitchen led to a grassy backyard. Griff followed the sound of Alix's giggles to the large willow tree located on the side of the property. Her carefree laughter surprised him. Though she'd taken to Mrs. Baxter, Alix remained reserved around the older woman. Griff's concern was diminished somewhat by the fact that his office was now located in the upstairs level of his two-family house. He'd open his practice next week. Should a problem arise, Alix would rarely be far from his sight.

Childlike laughter echoed in the air and Griff smiled. For once, life seemed to be looking up. He turned the corner of the house and stared. Alix sat cuddled in Chelsie Russell's lap. Chelsie's brown hair ruffled in the breeze and she looked down, struggling to keep the light wind from turning the pages of a book. That Alix's little fingers kept grabbing pages made the task more difficult.

"More." His niece's voice drifted towards him.

He stepped closer, mesmerized by the image of the woman reading to Alix, the little girl who had become the center of his being. With their heads bent forward, dark curls ruffled by the wind, they looked so alike they could have been mother and daughter.

Alix laughed, happier than any time in Griff's recent memory.

As he'd seen the last time they were together, something about Chelsie struck a chord in his niece. Whether it was Chelsie's resemblance to her sister or something more, Chelsie reached Alix where others could not. Watching them together, Griff silently acknowledged that this woman affected him, as well.

He remained quiet and listened to her soft voice. He searched his mind for similar images in his past, but none came. When his mother had taken off in search of a better, wealthier lifestyle, the task of raising Jared had fallen to Griff. His father tried, but juggling fatherhood and a full-time job had been difficult. As a child, Griff had been denied the uncomplicated pleasure of having a story read to him. When his little brother had gotten scared or lonely, Griff had made up exaggerated tales to distract him. No one had been there for Griff then.

For the moment, he let Chelsie's voice surround him. Absorbed in her tale, he allowed himself to pretend life could be different, that he could indulge in both love and trust without having them thrown back in his face.

"The end." Chelsie shut the book. Eyes closed, she lifted her face towards the sun. A peaceful expression touched her features, making her appear vulnerable. Soft and approachable, he thought. Almost as she had after the hearing, when she'd tried to apologize.

Reality intruded, unbidden and unwelcome. Griff forced himself to recall why he'd never have such a loving family scene in his own home. The pleasant feelings she invoked disappeared, along with his good mood. How could he have allowed himself to feel anything for Chelsie Russell?

"Having fun?" Careful not to upset Alix, he kept his voice neutral.

Chelsie's gaze met his. He couldn't decipher the

look in her eyes, though he'd like to think it was guilt.

"I was just reading Alix a story."

"So I see."

"Butterfly," Alix said, tossing the book towards him.

Griff knelt down and caught Alix as she flew into his arms. He chuckled at her wide smile and grass-stained knees. "Where's Mrs. Baxter?" he asked, looking over the little girl's head.

"When I got here, she had a headache. I offered to watch Alix for a while." Chelsie stood and wiped dirt and grass off her jeans, her long fingers brushing against the faded denim. The material molded to her slender legs—legs he could envision wrapped around him in a much more intimate setting.

He muttered a curse and tore his gaze away from temptation, setting Alix down beside him. "Come with me, squirt. I think there's milk and cookies in the kitchen." Confrontation could wait until he side-tracked his niece.

The little girl let out a squeal of delight and took off across the lawn. "I'll be back after I find Mrs. Baxter and get Alix settled." Without waiting for an answer, Griff turned and caught up with Alix.

His gut instinct told him Chelsie would still be there when he got back. He and Chelsie obviously had things to settle between them. Why else would she have come?

TWO

Griff returned from the house to find Chelsie leaning against the tree, her legs crossed at the ankles. "I wanted to see how you and Alix were getting along," she said without preamble.

"Did you satisfy your curiosity?"

"It was more than curiosity. More like genuine concern for my niece's welfare." Her clipped tone was at odds with the soothing manner she'd used with Alix.

He allowed himself one second to regret the change before reminding himself why distance between them was necessary. "There's a first time for everything," he muttered. "Last time you acted on your genuine concern, I almost lost my brother's child."

She ran her tongue along her full bottom lip and his eyes followed the movement. That he had the ability to make the hotshot attorney nervous gave him some small measure of satisfaction. Not that it dispelled the overwhelming sexual attraction, but at least it gave him something to focus on.

"I'd like to apologize again," she said. "My parents are . . . let's just say they're my parents, not my role models."

"Fine. Apology accepted." He said nothing more. A bird chirped in the distance. Griff let the silence turn from casual to uncomfortable and Chelsie shifted her weight from one foot to the other.

"Mrs. Baxter seems nice." She broke the silence first, but the tension remained.

"She is."

"Alix seems to like her."

"She does."

Apparently, his curt answers weren't a deterrent, because she didn't take the hint and leave. Griff didn't know how much longer he could fight both his anger and his hormones. As much as he disliked her, he found himself unwillingly attracted to Chelsie. He wasn't surprised. Where women were concerned, his judgment was decidedly poor.

"I think she enjoyed the time we spent together. When I got here, Mrs. Baxter was busy cooking dinner and Alix was playing alone."

"I see. So now she's being neglected."

"Are you always so defensive? I wasn't criticizing, just making an observation."

"In case you hadn't caught on, I've had it with your interference."

She paused, as if deliberating her next statement. Her tongue flicked over her lower lip again, and every ounce of willpower he possessed went into taking his eyes away from the sensual movement. Desire had no place in their relationship. Hell, they didn't even have a relationship.

And they never would.

Short of escorting her to the car, he could think of no way to get her out of here. But the conflicting emotions she touched off inside him were dangerous to his mental health.

"I meant my earlier offer to help out with Alix," she said, unwittingly giving him his escape route.

He pounced without hesitation. "Next time you feel the need to mother, have a kid of your own. I'll take care of Alix from now on."

Tears welled in her brown eyes and a corresponding pain filled his gut. One look at her expression and he almost reconsidered, almost took her up on her offer to help. But the part of him that had been so recently betrayed rebelled at the notion. And, he reminded himself, she'd already proven how little she cared for others.

So what was she doing here now? He pushed aside the nagging question that brought with it a flood of unwelcome guilt. He wanted to hurt her, and he had.

"I have a legal right to visit my niece," she said once she'd regained some of her composure.

He disliked the reminder. "Next time call first."

Her eyes narrowed, but to his surprise she didn't fight him. "Fine. Alix loved this story, so you might want to read it to her sometime." She handed him a worn, yellow book. "It's a little old for her, but she'll grow into it." Her voice cracked. She ducked her head in embarrassment and turned and ran for her car.

He glanced down at the book she'd shoved into his hand. He didn't recognize the title. Curious, he flipped through the tattered pages. Chelsie's name was scrawled in block letters on the inside flap. He slid down onto the grass to read.

Closing the front cover, he pondered the mystery

of Chelsie Russell. In court, she'd represented two people guaranteed to have a detrimental effect on Alix's life. Yet today, she'd given his niece a story about life, rebirth, and hope. Something to hold on to for the future, despite all she'd lost.

Chelsie had obviously saved the book from her own childhood. Had she turned these same pages when she felt alone? *Dammit, he shouldn't care.* He muttered another curse, then stood and headed inside.

Chelsie made the first right turn off Griffin's street and stopped the car at the curb, certain she was out of his sight. Still trembling, she shoved the gear shift to park and rested her head on the steering wheel. When she had decided to check on Alix, she had told herself to expect Griffin's anger or distrust. She realized now that she had counted on the passage of time to cool his ire. The barely concealed hatred that emanated from deep within him had taken her by surprise.

The hard look in Griffin's eyes, coupled with his callous words, had taken her back to another time, another place. Memories that lurked just beneath her consciousness had threatened to surface and destroy her hard-won emotional stability and calm. She centered herself with two simple words: *another man.*

Not Griffin. Regardless of the depth of his anger, he'd never lose control. He wasn't capable of physical abuse. She didn't know how she was so certain, just that she was. Perhaps the way he looked at his niece allowed her to believe in him despite his rough edges and harsh tone.

Her ex-husband had had more than rough edges

beneath the civilized veneer. He'd acted on his anger, reacted to whatever life dished out that didn't go his way—unlike Griffin, who accepted and tried to move on, she thought.

No, the two men were nothing alike. But that didn't make Griffin any less dangerous to her well-being. An attraction existed that she couldn't deny. His harsh exterior covered a gentler side. Heaven help her should she ever be the recipient of the kinder Griffin Stuart. Thankfully, that possibility didn't exist.

Though she'd like to pretend this was just another completed case and walk away, she couldn't turn her back on her sister's child. She wouldn't, regardless of the consequences. Being around Alix forced her to face the fact that her ex-husband's last violent act had assured her of an empty future and no children of her own.

Over the years following her marriage, she had learned to live in the present without getting mired in the past. Time, circumstance, and Griffin's careless words brought the past she thought she'd buried into the present. *Next time you feel the need to mother, have a kid of your own.*

She opened the car window, hoping the fresh air would clear her head. Today was an atypical August day. Instead of sweltering heat and humidity, the air felt cool, hinting at an early autumn. She normally looked forward to this particular change of seasons. For some, spring meant a time of renewal, but she preferred the fall. For Chelsie, autumn was memory free. At least it had been, until a little girl with dark hair had captured her heart . . . and the child's uncle had stomped on it.

She slammed her hand on the wheel in frustration. Since the day she'd accepted her fate, she'd never succumbed to tears or self-pity, and she cursed Griffin Stuart for forcing her to do so now. After taking a deep breath of fresh air, she felt better. She turned the key in the ignition, but before she drove off, she had to stop and wipe the tears that blurred her vision.

"Thanks for coming." Griff opened the front door for his friend.

"No problem." Ryan walked in, kicked off his shoes, and headed straight for the kitchen, where he opened the refrigerator and grabbed a can of cola.

"Make yourself at home," Griff said wryly.

Ryan grinned. "Already have."

Since they were kids, neighbors in a run-down apartment building, Ryan had always reached the fridge first, usually swiping the last can of soda, leaving only tap water for Griff. For Jared, Ryan would make an exception, letting him share the victor's spoils. Both Griff and Ryan had looked out for the pesky kid they both thought of as a little brother.

Ryan gave his friend the once over. "You look like hell," he said between gulps.

Griff ran his fingers through his disheveled hair. "Feel like it, too."

"Did you get her back to sleep?"

"Yeah." He followed Ryan back to the living room. "But since it's the third time, I don't hold out much hope of her sleeping through the night." Griff glanced towards the clock on the fireplace mantel.

A picture of his brother and sister-in-law, taken at Alix's first birthday, drew his attention, mocking his efforts at parenting. *I'm sorry I'm letting you down.* He turned his gaze to the clock at the right of the picture.

Almost midnight. His body ached, whether from lack of sleep or bending over the crib to soothe his niece, he didn't know. His heart ached, as well, but at least he could attribute that to a direct source. He glanced back at the photo.

"I shouldn't be surprised," Griff said, forcing his thoughts to his present problem. "This night isn't much different than any other in the past month or so."

No sooner would he fall asleep than he'd be awakened by Alix's piercing cries. The doctor attributed the problem to her strange surroundings and the absence of her parents. Though he assured Griff that in time things would settle down, they hadn't. They'd gotten worse.

"Isn't your live-in help working out?" Ryan asked.

"Mrs. Baxter offered to help out at night, but then she'd be useless during the day. As it is, I'm sure she's not catching much sleep just by virtue of proximity. Anyway, Alix needs someone familiar. Right now, that's me."

Ryan flopped onto the sofa, his second cola in hand. "And me. Get out. I can handle things from here. I'm used to being up all night on assignment, and I've had my caffeine fix." He waved the can in the air. "You need the sleep. No way you'll function in court if you're sleeping through the proceedings."

"Appreciate it, buddy. I owe you."

"Yeah. Ain't life grand?" Ryan grinned.

"It's been better."

"Haven't you gotten one decent night's sleep since the squirt moved in?"

"No."

Ryan snorted in disbelief. "Pretty quick answer. Are you sure you wouldn't like to reconsider?"

"You're a pain in the butt, Jackson."

"Maybe. But how about some honesty? I seem to remember your mentioning one particular night when you thought you had the problem beat."

"If you know so much, then why ask the damned question?"

"Because friends make you face things you don't want to own up to." Ryan kicked off his shoes and propped his feet up on the sofa. "So?"

"So, yes. One night last week Alix slept. I didn't." Since the day Chelsie had run from his home in tears, he had lived with a steady and conflicting diet of guilt and desire. His fluctuating feelings regarding Chelsie Russell kept him up nights, so the one evening Alix chose to sleep, Griff tossed and turned.

The battle had been hell on him, physically as well as emotionally. A fair exchange, given how badly he'd treated Chelsie. Yet given a second chance, he'd do the same thing all over again. Self-preservation at its finest.

"Aha," Ryan muttered.

"Don't *aha* me. I'm going to bed."

"If you ask me, both you and Alix need her."

"We have each other, Ryan. We don't need anyone else." Especially a woman capable of turning his life upside down. He'd seen firsthand the lengths to which Chelsie would go to get something she wanted. No different than Deidre or his so-called mother. Regardless of Chelsie's effect on him—and he couldn't deny he felt something each time he even thought of Chelsie Russell—he didn't want to add her to his already convoluted life.

"Strand yourself on a deserted island, and you'll wind up alone." Ryan flicked on the television set.

"Excuse me if I don't stick around and listen to you spout philosophy. I've got some sleep to catch up on." Griff turned and headed for the door.

"Pleasant dreams."

Griff ignored Ryan's jibe and low chuckle. His friend's poor sense of humor was a small thing to overlook in favor of a good night's sleep.

He entered his bedroom and stripped off his clothing, collapsing onto the cool sheets in exhaustion. He expected sleep to come immediately, but he lay awake with one thing on his mind. Chelsie Russell.

Until now, he had refused to contemplate the connection between Alix's well-being and her aunt, the complex lady lawyer who tormented his dreams.

Chelsie's parents were no longer interested in Alix. Since the hearing a month ago, they had stopped by only once. Because the judge's ruling had reiterated the importance of family ties and deep down Griff agreed, he'd been willing to allow the Russells supervised family visits. Apparently, having discovered that the judge's decision hadn't affected their status with the country club set, their granddaughter no longer fit into their plans. No need to burden themselves with a child if their shallow friends accepted them anyway.

A part of him acknowledged the possibility that Chelsie's parents were grief-stricken and upset over losing custody on top of losing a daughter. That didn't justify ignoring the same child whose life they had tried to turn upside down. Regardless of the reason for their absence, Griff wasn't surprised, merely relieved.

Thankfully, Alix didn't know the difference. Her restless nights were constant with or without her grandparents' presence in her life. Chelsie was a different story. Whether Griff liked it or not, and he definitely did not, Alix responded to her. Chelsie obviously created a sense of security the little girl lacked otherwise. That the cold lady lawyer could do for his niece what Griff could not aggravated him. He'd like to think the one peaceful night in a troubled month was mere coincidence. But deep down, he knew better. The child's smiles and giggles had been freer around Chelsie.

He punched the pillow and lay down with an arm tucked beneath his head. The one person Griff needed to stay away from was the one person Alix needed to put her on the road to emotional recovery. His niece had to take priority over his own feelings.

But could he be around Chelsie and not replay her role in the custody battle, not compare her to the selfish women in his past, his mother and fiancée? He thought about the tattered yellow book Alix carried around with her and exhaled deeply. Chelsie fit the mold . . . and yet she didn't.

Alix's cries pierced the night. Griff was halfway out of bed before he remembered Ryan was on duty. He lay back onto the mattress and groaned aloud.

Chelsie Russell. Could he be around her and not want her? He was about to find out.

* * *

Chelsie turned on the television and inserted an exercise video into the VCR. She preferred her own company to the patrons of the health club around the corner from her office. Her secretary and next-door neighbor, always a reliable source, had informed her that most women went there to meet eligible men. Since Chelsie had decided to steer clear of the male species, her apartment was as good a place as any for working out.

She secured a rubber band around her hair and unlocked the door for her neighbor. Though an efficient worker, her secretary was always late and sometimes a no-show for their exercise sessions. Since Chelsie had spent the last two days tied up in court, her friend's schedule was anybody's guess. Chelsie decided to start without her.

She began with a tough series of stretches before settling in for serious relaxation. After such a long day, she could use both. Almost running into Griffin Stuart hadn't helped. She raised her right arm above her head and counted aloud. "And one . . . and two . . ." Though she knew Griffin had begun working out of his home, she hadn't figured him for a family-court type of practitioner. After his go-for-the-jugular display the other day, she'd pretty much decided he'd stick to cut-throat litigation or hard-ball corporate law. She lowered her right arm and lifted her left. "And one . . . and two . . ."

Dealing with broken families and children required a heart. Though he displayed his heart for Alix, Chelsie had seen Griffin's other side. In an effort to avoid him, she'd headed for the nearest door. When she ended up in the cafeteria, she succumbed to a chocolate craving. Now she was working off both stress and sweets, courtesy of a man who obviously didn't understand the meaning of forgiveness.

Leg lifts, she decided, as she raised her right leg in the air, were more painful when she skipped a week between sessions. She ought to cut back on her caseload, but knew better than to think she could turn away a needy client. Despite her heavy breathing, she felt good, as if she were exorcising all the demons that Griffin Stuart had brought back into her life.

Experience had taught Chelsie to learn her lesson the first time. "I'm sorry" only counted when the person uttering the words had the ability and the desire not to repeat his mistakes. "I didn't mean it" was the coward's way of not accepting responsibility for his actions. Chelsie had believed her husband one too many times. She'd stayed in her marriage and paid the ultimate price. Abuse wasn't only physical, and one such relationship was one too many.

With Griffin, she'd slipped, but never again. She didn't intend to give him a third chance to insult her. Nor did she want to be reminded of her own painful past, something he'd managed to do quite easily and without much remorse. No, she could find time to see her niece when he wasn't around.

She tucked a stray strand of hair back into her ponytail, switched sides and lifted her left leg. Chelsie didn't need another slap in the face. She'd made a huge mistake. She'd also apologized. His penetrating eyes and sexy looks didn't entitle him to treat her like dirt.

He wasn't worth another thought.

So why have you wasted an entire workout session obsessing about him? She wouldn't dignify that thought with an answer. Chelsie lowered her leg, lay down on her back, and began the deep breathing session of the tape.

"Hello?" Griff knocked lightly and pushed the door open further. Though he felt like an intruder, he entered anyway and peered inside. One glance at Chelsie stretched out on the floor and he rushed in, kneeling beside her for a closer look.

Her chest rose and fell in steady intervals. Once he realized she was okay, he noticed more than her even breathing. A cranberry-colored bodysuit and tights molded her lithe body. With each breath she took, her full breasts became more evident. Damp tendrils of hair clung to her slender neck. His body hardened at the sight. She looked sated. The word brought sensual images to mind. Images of those long legs wrapped around him as he . . .

What the hell was wrong with him? He tore his gaze from her body and noticed the T.V. had faded to black-and-white fuzz. Grateful for the diversion, he popped the tape out of the VCR and shut down both it and the television. He glanced at the video in his hand. "Exercise and Relaxation." He shook his head in disbelief. She'd fallen asleep mid-exercise with her door open and unlocked.

His gaze drifted to her sleeping form. Her cheeks were flushed pink from exertion, her full lips parted slightly in repose. With a shake of his head, he tried to clear his thoughts. He'd have to do better if he intended to have her around. For Alix's sake, he had no choice. He snorted in disgust.

The sound woke her. She took one look at him

leaning over her and let out an ear-piercing shriek, loud enough to deafen him for life.

"Calm down. I'm not a stranger." Stupid words, but what else could he say to a woman whose apartment he had entered uninvited and whom he had wakened from a sound sleep? Especially when he was fairly certain he wouldn't be welcome under ordinary circumstances.

She scrambled to her knees and scurried backwards, placing a large distance between them. Her eyes seemed wide and unfocused. Fear. She appeared paralyzed by the emotion. If he wasn't mistaken, she didn't recognize him.

"Chelsie?" He reached out a hand and gently touched her shoulder, his fingertips connecting with her silken skin.

She shook her head and strands of hair fell from their binding. As if in response to his touch, her gaze focused on him, awareness dawning slowly in her dark eyes. "Griff?" she asked in a shaky but husky voice.

His name on her lips sounded incredibly intimate. She'd never called him by name before, especially not the abbreviated version used by his close friends. He was surprised she did so now.

"Can I help you up?"

She grasped his extended hand and allowed him to pull her to a standing position. Her palm felt cold and clammy, similar to Alix's forehead when she awakened in fright. Given his unexpected appearance in her apartment, he supposed Chelsie's response was normal, yet he couldn't help wondering if there was more to her reaction than just shock.

Intending to lead her to the couch, he placed one

hand on the small of her back. This time, she stiffened at his touch and pivoted around to glare at him. "What the hell are you doing in my apartment?"

"For a supposedly smart woman, you aren't too bright. You live in the city of Boston and fall asleep on the floor with your door wide open. Anyone could come in. Anyone could see you lying on your back, half dressed, ready for heaven knows what . . ."

A deep flush crept up her neck and stained her cheeks. "Well, don't be subtle about expressing yourself." She turned her back to him and picked up an old gray sweatshirt, pulling it over her upper body, effectively hiding her sexy shape from his view. "Excuse me for a minute," she said and disappeared into another room.

As his gaze swept the expanse of the small living area, he noticed his surroundings for the first time. Crystal animals and fragile ornaments accented an otherwise sleek decor comprised mostly of leather and glass. Hardly a place for a child. At least he'd left Alix at home with Mrs. Baxter. He'd hate to think of the damage a little girl could do in such an environment.

Griff picked up a crystal rabbit and fingered its smooth contours. Miss Russell obviously loved fine things. He thought of his mother, of the expensive pieces she'd bring home after a romp with one of her many men. "A woman wants more out of life," she'd told him on the afternoon Griff had watched her pack. "And your daddy can't give it to me. But I'll find it, just you wait."

She'd looked around before closing her tattered suitcase, her eyes focusing on the chipped coffee table in the center of the room. And Griff, like the twelve-year-old child he'd been, had thought she'd take the picture of himself and Jared, that she'd be back. Instead, her hand grasped a perfume bottle, one of the many objects she'd used to flaunt her affairs before his father. Griff had been wrong on both counts. And Chelsie, it seemed, was similar to his mother and ex-fiancée, sharing their love of possessions and probably valuing them above people.

This visit had been a mistake. She couldn't help Alix. He wanted to turn and run before she returned. He nearly did, until his eyes focused on the bookshelf in the corner. Mixed in with the expensive trinkets were a set of books worn by use and age. A gap between two of the volumes indicated one was missing. He thought of Alix and the death-grip she kept on the damned yellow story book. There it was again—Chelsie Russell and her contradictions.

She cleared her throat. With a sound that was half sigh, half groan, he faced her. She'd covered her long legs with baggy sweats that matched the oversized sweatshirt. Unfortunately, instead of sexy, she now looked soft and cuddly. Neither helped Griff's frame of mind.

"The rabbit's my favorite," she said.

He frowned and replaced the animal.

"Getting back to your point." She gestured towards the door. "As it happens, I live in a high-security building. And the door was unlocked, not open."

"Like a burglar or rapist would have recognized the difference," he said. "And it must have opened while you slept."

"Oh." She looked down, apparently duly chastised.

At least he'd made his point about her safety.

Suddenly, she glanced up, her dark eyes narrowing suspiciously. "Just how did you get up here without the doorman calling first?"

"I latched onto a large party headed for another floor. I didn't think you'd be too receptive if I called ahead."

"Good thinking."

"And if I could do that, so could anyone."

"Point taken. I'll be more careful in the future, though I was expecting company."

Male or female? None of your damned business. This evening was not going as he'd planned. Both his thoughts and his actions were betraying him. He needed to focus on the purpose of his visit and not his past . . . or her impossibly long legs. "Good," he muttered.

"What do you want?" she asked.

You. He shook his head in pure frustration. Focus, he reminded himself. "Look, I realize I frightened you and I'm sorry."

She crossed her arms over her chest. "Apology accepted."

The silence in the small apartment overwhelmed him. Obviously, she intended to make him pay for his rude behavior last week. Anything for Alix, he thought, and prepared to grovel.

THREE

Chelsie glanced at her surprise visitor, who obviously planned on taking his time before revealing why he had come. Resigned to a drawn-out conversation, she lifted her arms, then let them fall to her side. "Have a seat."

So far he'd done nothing more than berate her bad judgment. Now that she thought about it, though, her open-door policy with her neighbor wasn't smart. Safety was a state she'd worked hard to achieve, one she couldn't afford to risk by being careless. A security guard sat at the only entrance to the building and, given the small number of apartments on each floor, each guard knew every tenant by name. Chelsie felt secure here, which was why she'd chosen the building. Obviously, she hadn't shut the door completely. In the future, she'd try to be more careful.

When she'd awakened to the sight of a man standing over her, she'd almost passed out. Such an overwhelming reaction hadn't happened to her in years. Griffin Stuart had an uncanny knack of bringing up the worst memories of her life, but she couldn't fault him for coincidence, only for his abominable behavior. Which made her wonder again what he wanted.

"Drink?" she asked, recognizing he wouldn't be rushed.

He shook his head. She curled into the corner of an oversized chair and motioned toward the couch.

"Thanks." He sat across from her, leaning forward on his elbows. "You're more gracious than I've been."

"That's an understatement. What can I do for you?"

He rubbed a hand wearily over his face. For the first time, she really looked at him. Dark circles shadowed his eyes and razor stubble covered his face. He looked depleted, exhausted, and yet incredibly sexy. Heat curled in the pit of her stomach, followed by a rush of surprise.

She hadn't reacted to a man in years. She'd thought sexual desire had died along with her marriage and unborn child. Apparently, Griff brought out more than just memories of her past. He made her feel desire and need. Those were sensations she'd buried long ago and didn't dare resurrect. She wished he would get to the point of his visit.

"I need a favor," he finally said. "And after your role in the custody hearing, I figure you owe me one."

Both curiosity and need vanished, replaced by anger at his high-handed tone. *"I owe you?"* She shook her head, unable to believe his nerve. "Try asking me without laying on the guilt. I've already apologized not once but twice. I've been insulted. I've been told in no uncertain terms to stay away from you and *my* niece. And, if you'll recall, I've been practically thrown out of your home. So if you think I haven't paid for taking the damned case, think again."

She paused for a steadying breath. Since losing custody, her own parents hadn't been forgiving either, having retreated to sunny Florida to "heal." She'd never been particularly close with either parent, which was why she'd tried so hard after her sister's death to bring her family together. Thanks to her conscience, she'd been paying for that misguided attempt ever since.

Griff's continuing hostility bothered her more than her own flesh and blood's, and more than she cared to admit. She met his gaze. "Under the circumstances, I've treated you a hell of a lot better than you've treated me. Now. I'll ask you again. What can I do for you?"

He gulped hard, causing his Adam's apple to bob up and down. Chelsie wondered if he'd swallowed his pride.

His light eyes reflected some inner torment and drew her in deeper than was prudent.

"I need you," he grudgingly admitted. "I mean, I need your help with Alix." Griff steeled himself, waiting for Chelsie's I-told-you-so reaction.

He hadn't exactly handled this evening with finesse, so he figured she'd take advantage of having the upper hand. After all the grief he'd given her, he fully expected her to grab the opportunity.

"What's wrong? Is Alix okay?"

He narrowed his gaze. "That's it? No, 'I told you so'?"

"Is that what you want? There are more important things at stake here than who's right and who's wrong. Is Alix okay?" she asked again, with what sounded like genuine concern.

"Yes. And no." Chelsie had managed to put him in his place and make him feel petty without resorting to feminine tactics. No tears, no theatrics, just honesty. Though impressed, he warned himself to proceed with caution. He'd been duped before.

"Which is it?" she asked.

"A little of both." He launched into a detailed description of his nights during the time Alix had been in his care, a summary that included a lot of floor walking and little sleep. "Except for the day you stopped by. That afternoon and evening, she was the child I remembered. The one my brother and your sister raised. I'm desperate enough to chance that it wasn't a coincidence. So I'd like you to spend time with her. Visit on a regular basis."

Her dark eyes widened at his request. He reminded himself that he'd had more than a few days to adjust to this idea. She'd had one second. If her offer to help had been sincere, he'd have no problem. If, on the other hand, her offer had been phony, a passing thought to soothe a guilty conscience, he'd best find out before any harm was done to Alix.

"Evenings at the house, suppers," he explained. "Just help create a stable environment. Once she's sleeping better, you'd be off the hook."

She shook her head, causing her ponytail to swish with the force of the movement. "I can't."

"You mean you won't." He refused to admit she'd disappointed him again. He'd known all along that Chelsie had nothing to gain by helping him. Despite her claims to care about Alix's welfare, her initial interest in his niece had been for the sole purpose of helping her parents and reaping any professional rewards that entailed. After all, her parents had influential friends who could be persuaded to hire a new attorney.

Maybe she'd even suffered a momentary pang of guilt for the distance she'd placed between herself and her sister. Maybe not. For all he knew, her visit to his home could have been at her parents' request, as well.

"I mean I can't."

"Doesn't matter. Semantics aside, it all amounts to the same thing. No is no." He braced his hand on the arm of the leather sofa and pushed himself to a standing position. "Thanks for your time." Without a good-bye, he headed for the door.

"Hold it." Her voice caught him before he'd reached the hallway.

He turned to find her right behind him and reached out to grasp her upper arms before she barreled into him. Awareness flickered in her eyes at the unexpected contact. Her startled expression and flushed cheeks betrayed her inner feelings. He'd thought himself alone in this vortex of tangled emotions. That she felt the same desire shocked him.

The heat of her flesh coursed through his fingertips, despite the layers of clothing. Firm yet soft— another Chelsie Russell contradiction. This one caused his body to come alive. The desire to dip his head and taste the lips that had opened in surprise surged through him.

Before he could rethink the wisdom of his actions, he lowered his head to taste what she seemed to offer. His mouth met hers and her lips softened in acceptance.

His hands roamed over her. Even through the barrier of clothing, he could feel every curve. He exhaled, and his next breath was filled with her enticing scent, making his fists clench and his groin harden in unmistakable need.

Griff wanted more than a simple kiss. He wanted Chelsie. With that notion, stark reality and the reasons for his visit came flooding back hard and fast. His fingers, which he'd wrapped around her sweatshirt, uncurled as he released his hold and stepped back.

Chelsie simply stared, her moist lips mocking his current attempt at restraint. He'd been a damned fool, responding to a woman who angered him beyond belief, who made flippant offers to help and reneged when faced with the reality of her words, who toyed with a child's life. With that reminder, he backed as far away as the small hallway would allow.

"Well?" he asked, letting impatience spark in his voice. Better than the sparks that had flown just seconds earlier. Their physical attraction was an inconsequential but annoying fact, one he could ignore with enough willpower. After her easy rejection of his niece and her problems, that shouldn't be too hard. Or so he told himself, knowing he'd spend a ridiculous amount of time trying to convince himself of that fact.

"Well what?" she asked in a none-too-steady voice.

"I was on my way out. You followed. I assume you wanted something?"

She flushed a deep crimson at his choice of words. To her credit, though, she ignored his sarcasm.

"Come back and sit down," she said. "We aren't finished yet." She folded her arms across her chest and met his steady gaze.

"I have my answer."

"But not my reasons. I intend to give them to you,

so sit down and listen for once." She brushed past him, shaking her head as she walked. Her decidedly feminine scent lingered in the air, hitting him like a blow to his midsection. Lilacs? He suppressed a groan. Chelsie Russell gave new meaning to this concept of self-control.

She cleared her throat, and he met her gaze. From the center of the living room, she motioned for him to join her. "How do you practice law if you haven't learned to listen?" she asked.

He listened—to everyone except Chelsie. With her, he reacted without thinking. That included leaping to unflattering conclusions without regard to the facts. Even when he heard what she had to say, he dismissed her words as meaningless.

Yet he had gone so far as to ask for her help. He had passed the contemplation stage and had actually wanted to have her around his niece, so he must have sensed some thread of decency in her nature. Despite what had just passed between them, she was right. He did owe her the chance to explain.

He groaned and followed her back inside to reclaim his position on the couch. "I'm listening."

"Okay." She leaned forward in her seat. "There's a lot more involved with your request than you realize. Asking me to give you a regimented schedule wouldn't work for any of us."

All business. She'd obviously put their encounter aside with ease. Just as he intended to do. So why did he find his gaze drawn to her still flushed face?

"My life is . . . let's just say it's complicated," she said.

"How so?"

"My career. I work twelve-, sometimes fifteen-hour

days, weekends included. Even then, my desk backs up."

That she'd put her practice before her own niece shouldn't surprise him. She'd hardly spent much time with the little girl before now. But he could overcome this objection with ease. "You could come by for supper. You'd have to eat anyway."

"At my desk, or on the run. As it is, I have to refer more clients than I like. Long dinners would put me even further behind." Sound reasoning, but for some reason, she couldn't meet his gaze. Perhaps she wasn't as confident in rejecting him as she'd like him to believe.

Sure as Alix would suffer from another restless night, Griff knew he would regret this. But the words escaped before he could think them through. "I could take on some of your work, lighten your caseload."

She stared. "I couldn't ask you . . ."

"You didn't. I'm offering."

"Why?"

Beats the hell out of me. From the day he'd faced off against Chelsie Russell in the courtroom until the moment he'd kissed her tonight, nothing in his life had made sense. Why should it start now?

"For Alix," he said. "Your niece." If Chelsie's excuses were sincere and he solved every one, she'd have no reason to turn him down. Suddenly, her acquiescence became important to him for reasons other than Alix. Reasons he wouldn't put into words.

"I don't know."

"Think about it."

"Work aside, I have other obligations to consider. Not more important, but they do exist."

Obligations, he thought with a strange mixture of dismay and frustration. And a tinge of jealousy? "Couldn't you explain to your boyfriend or significant other that you were doing a favor for a friend?"

She grinned, a teasing glint replacing the serious shadow in her eyes. "So you've elevated me to the status of friend? I'm flattered."

"I meant Alix."

"She's family." Her lips lifted again and a light chuckle escaped.

"Well?" he asked.

"Unlike you, some of us have obligations other than the social kind."

"What kind of remark is that?" Since the day of his brother's accident, his life had revolved around a two-year-old sprite, her whims and tantrums. Social obligations didn't factor into the equation.

"Your reputation precedes you."

"Do you always believe what you hear?"

"No, but coupled with my parents' information . . ."

"And because they're your parents, of course you believe them." Since their lies had been exposed in court, he grunted at the notion. "Haven't you learned your lesson?"

"You're right." She sighed.

Something in her voice told him she understood her parents better than he'd realized. Coupled with the fact that she didn't lead their wealthy, self-centered lifestyle, but had made her way on her own, he believed her.

He leaned forward in his seat.

"I'm sorry for prying," she said. "But you did begin this inquiry into personal matters. Can't blame me for playing the same game."

"A little girl's life isn't a game."

"That isn't what I meant and you know it."

Truth be told, he did. "Look, I was engaged and it didn't work out. Last I heard, a monogamous relationship couldn't be classified as having an active social life." When had this turned into a foray into *his* personal life? And why had he chosen to confide even a sparse summary to Chelsie Russell?

He shook his head. "Back to you. Couldn't you put whatever it is on hold for a while?"

"Absolutely not." With another sigh, she released her hair from its binding. She ran her fingers through the tangled strands. "I said I'd like to help with Alix, but I didn't envision a scheduled commitment, one that she'd come to rely on." Her expressive eyes glazed over and she looked beyond him to a picture on the wall.

Another woman who couldn't handle the complications of both Griff and his niece. He should have known better than to think he could change Chelsie's mind. All the cajoling and mutual desire in the world wouldn't alter the status quo.

"I've got to get back to Alix. I heard your reasons and I accept them. Thanks anyway." Exhaustion overcame him, seeping in like a familiar but unwelcome visitor. He'd groveled enough for one evening, and he still had to make it through another sleepless night.

Chelsie followed him down the small entryway, holding the door open as he stepped into the hall. If he didn't know better, he'd think she looked distraught. But he had to be mistaken. Of the two of them, he'd been the one put through the emotional wringer tonight. She'd merely had the pleasure of watching.

" 'Night, Chelsie." He strode toward the bank of elevators.

"Griff?"

At the sound of her soft voice, he turned. "Yes?" A glimmer of hope flickered to life inside him.

She opened her mouth to speak, then shut it again, shaking her head instead. Alone in the empty hallway, she appeared small and frail, in need of protection, of his arms wrapped around her slender waist. The elevator door opened, preventing him from acting on his unwanted desires.

Griff steeled himself against his warring emotions and stepped inside without looking back. He leaned against the grimy wall and punched the lobby key with more force than necessary.

When would he learn? Though he thought he'd lost his ability to trust, part of him must have foolishly believed in Chelsie or else he wouldn't have come. He'd sensed an emotional connection between his niece and the lady lawyer. Alix's aunt, he reminded himself.

As a result, he'd nurtured a silent wish that Chelsie would turn out to be different from the other women he'd known.

He stifled a bitter laugh. Chelsie wasn't different, just better at stringing him along. She had no more interest in Alix than her parents had.

Chelsie's hands shook as she poured herself a cup of herbal tea. Any residual effects of her relaxation session were long gone. Stress and tension coiled every muscle in her body. The look of disappointment in Griff's eyes had nearly destroyed her.

When had his opinion begun to count? When she kissed him? Felt the length of his body pressed against hers? Or when she'd responded to him in a way she'd never felt before?

She lifted the mug and the tea sloshed over the side. *Men aren't supposed to matter, dammit.* But this one did and so did her niece. How could she tell him the truth, that she feared developing an emotional bond with Alix—and Griff—only to have them ripped from her at his whim? Regardless of the fact that he needed her now, they'd part in the end. His abrupt ending to the kiss, something she should have done much sooner, assured her of that.

She'd always be a peripheral part of Alix's life. She wanted a relationship with her sister's little girl. But if she allowed herself to be a daily part of Alix's life, if she allowed herself to become truly attached, the resulting emptiness would be like reliving her own worst nightmare. Her miscarriage and the abuse that precipitated it had been traumatic enough, but the doctor's pronouncement that she'd never have another baby had shattered her dreams and changed her life. She'd learned not to hope for what couldn't be.

Griff and Alix were a ready-made family, the type of family Chelsie would never have. Knowingly placing herself in a position that guaranteed emotional pain was plain stupid. She'd done the right thing. She would still see her niece, but on her terms. Safe terms.

Yet the look in Griff's eyes . . . he and Alix were suffering. Though Chelsie doubted she represented the solution Griff so desperately needed, he believed she did, enough to put aside his lingering doubts and place Alix in her care. That sort of trust ought to mean something, she thought, coming no closer to a decision.

How could she place her heart in such jeopardy? How could she not?

Dusk was beginning to fall when Chelsie pulled up to the big house with the freshly painted white picket fence surrounding the front yard. Potted red geraniums, just beginning to flower, lined the three front steps leading to the screened-porch door. A child couldn't pick a more cheerful place to grow up, which, Chelsie surmised, was why Griff had chosen it. Cliched but perfect, nevertheless.

She took the bluestone walkway at a brisk pace, afraid she might turn and run otherwise. Not only was this house a child's dream, but a family couldn't find a more comforting place to build memories.

Mrs. Baxter let her in with a huge smile and warm welcome and directed Chelsie to follow her inside.

"Admit it, you coward. You aren't afraid of his reaction to your showing up without calling again. You're afraid his offer is still open," Chelsie muttered to herself.

"Did you say something?" The older woman stopped halfway down the hall and turned to Chelsie.

"I said I'm sorry to keep showing up unexpectedly." She forced a smile.

"Nonsense. Just follow me. They're in here." Mrs. Baxter gestured toward an arched entryway. "You're just what this family needs."

Her words propelled Chelsie into motion. She pivoted on her heels, intending to hightail it back to her car. She could be safely ensconced in her office by eight. Work still needed to be done. Never put off until tomorrow what you can do today. Wasn't there a saying like that?

She had taken one step when Mrs. Baxter called a halt to her cowardly retreat. "Alix, someone special's here to see you."

Chelsie had nowhere to run or hide. Reluctantly, she turned back again.

"She doesn't let that book you brought her out of her sight," the woman said, a kind smile etching her features.

"Oh." Chelsie's legs felt wobbly. She'd passed the point where she could exit gracefully. Drawing a deep breath, she followed Mrs. Baxter into the kitchen. She only hoped Griff's mood was brighter than her own.

"I said eat it, don't throw it."

Chelsie stopped in the doorway and stared in disbelief as Griff wiped mashed potatoes off his face and shirt collar.

"Let's try this again, squirt." He scooped up another spoonful and attempted to feed Alix, who grabbed his hand mid-air, frustrating his efforts. "I'm warning you. The next time the food misses your stomach, it goes in the garbage."

Chelsie knew, just as Griff probably did, that reasoning with a two year old was as futile as reasoning with a stubborn client. Still, watching him attempt just that with more patience than she would have believed he possessed, endeared him to her at once. The bachelor with the carefree reputation had managed to surprise and impress her yet again.

The spoonful reached the little girl's mouth, but

instead of swallowing, Alix grinned and squirted the food back through her lips. Griff groaned, tossing a towel on the high chair in a gesture of defeat. "I give up. If you're pulling these stunts, you can't be hungry."

Chelsie suppressed the urge to laugh at the way the child had manipulated the man.

"Mrs. Baxter." He didn't call quietly, he bellowed.

"Right here, Mr. Stuart." He whirled around at the sound of the older woman's soft-spoken voice. "Sorry. I didn't hear you come in."

"I know. You were otherwise engaged."

"Would you mind cleaning her up while I work on myself?"

Nothing short of a shower would help, Chelsie thought. Without warning, images of a strong body and rivulets of water dripping over naked skin invaded her mind. She attempted to push aside the sensual images she'd evoked, but Griff hindered her effort.

Though he still wore trousers from his day at work, he'd stripped to his T-shirt, giving Chelsie a glimpse of muscles that flexed with each movement. She remembered the feel of those hard muscles beneath her fingertips. She had a hard time tearing her gaze from the sight and wished he hadn't chosen to save his shirt and tie from the little girl's perfect aim.

"I'd like to see her eat more," Mrs. Baxter said. Griff nodded in agreement.

Nothing could have distracted Chelsie faster than the chaos before her. She focused on her niece, who was no more cooperative with her baby-sitter than she'd been with her uncle.

The little girl's lips remained tightly closed. Mrs. Baxter and Griff exchanged frustrated looks. Because of Alix, the older woman had forgotten Chelsie's presence. She stood in the entryway and enjoyed the show. She hadn't wanted to call attention to herself any sooner than necessary, but the residents of this house obviously needed help. This adorable but feisty child knew which buttons to push on each adult to get her way.

"Maybe I could give it a try," Chelsie said.

"How did you get in?" Griff turned around as he spoke.

"Well, good evening to you, too." Undaunted, she walked over to where Alix sat, rubbing the potatoes and whatever else had been made for dinner into her high-chair tray.

"Oh, I'm sorry. I forgot. Mr. Stuart, Miss Russell is here to see you and Alix."

"I realize that now." Griff smiled at the older woman, putting her at ease. "Why don't you call it a day?" He spoke to Mrs. Baxter, but looked at Chelsie. "Miss Russell and I can take things from here. Can't we?"

His direct gaze unnerved her. Alix's antics had distracted her from the purpose of this visit, but Griff brought her smack into reality. The man had a way of doing that to her in more ways than one.

Mrs. Baxter hesitated. "If you're sure."

"We're sure," they answered in unison. Chelsie didn't want an audience for round three with Griffin Stuart.

After kissing Alix good night, the older woman headed for her room.

"Let's see what you've got." He handed Chelsie a sticky bowl and gestured to the child in the high chair.

She accepted the challenge in silence. As the evening wore on, Chelsie not only coaxed Alix to finish her meal, but got her to behave in the bath. A silent agreement had been reached. All that remained was for them to work out the details. Regardless of the specifics, however, she intended to draw an imaginary boundary, one she wouldn't cross no matter what the circumstances.

This seemed like a good place to start. She stood in the doorway to Alix's bedroom. Under the glow of a small Mickey Mouse night-light, Chelsie made out Griff's large form leaning over the little girl's crib. Though lost in shadows, his movements were brisk, sure, and gentle.

Yes, Chelsie acknowledged, gentleness emanated from deep within him. She'd sensed his basic decency even when he'd treated her without regard to her own feelings. She'd felt it in the warm, deep giving of his kiss.

Without warning, he glanced over his shoulder, meeting her gaze. Locked in an understanding they themselves had created, Chelsie found herself unable to look away. The currents in the air changed suddenly. A frisson of awareness invaded her body, and she turned away in shock and embarrassment. When she'd centered herself, she turned back, but Griff's attention had refocused on Alix. Having such a heated reaction to his glance, Chelsie couldn't help but wonder what it would be like to be the sole focus of his gentle attention. A longing so strong it threatened to choke her arose.

"Say good night to Chelsie." Griff's deep voice penetrated her need.

The little girl mumbled something unintelligible and Griff tucked her in. Chelsie laughed, but tears blurred her vision as she watched from a safe distance. She refused the urge to aid in the nightly ritual of placing Alix in her crib, covering her with an old blanket, ruffling her dark curls, and kissing her good night. Motherly gestures invoked motherly feelings. If she helped, she would be lost—lost in a past she couldn't change, and a future she would never have.

Chelsie drew a steadying breath. Talcum powder, shampoo, and other baby smells permeated the air. She wrapped her arms around herself to ward off a sudden shiver. An empty and fruitless gesture, since the chill came from deep inside her heart.

Griff walked to where Chelsie stood. He placed a hand on the small of her back. She *knew* he only meant to lead her out of the room. But his touch set off hundreds of tiny explosions in body parts she'd long forgotten existed . . . and in parts she'd never been aware of before. Even her skin tingled.

Another shiver shook her, this one warm and friendly. As if he realized the reaction he'd caused and regretted the contact, he withdrew his hand. She drew a deep breath and preceded him out of the room.

They'd begun as adversaries and were now unwilling allies. She wondered if they'd ever get past the uneasy distrust that plagued their relationship. Perhaps it was best they never did. Friendly adversaries might be all she could hope for. At least then she'd stand a chance of keeping her heart intact.

FOUR

"Sorry to have kept you waiting."

Chelsie turned, startled at the sound of Griff's deep voice. Having retreated to the living room, she'd gotten lost in a file she'd retrieved from the car. No sense in wasting valuable free time, and what better way to tamp down unwanted emotions than by burying herself in work?

She closed the paperwork and placed it on the cushion beside her. "Not a problem. How could I begrudge a dirty man a shower?"

"Feeding Alix is an experience," he said, laughing.

Laughing? In the time since the hearing, Chelsie couldn't recall Griff treating her to a simple smile.

He ran his fingers through still damp hair as he entered the room, coming up beside her. She'd always thought him good looking, despite his brooding intensity. Now a relaxed grin transformed him into a different man. A small scar near his left eye crinkled when he smiled. Deep grooves surrounded dimples she'd never realized he possessed. She assumed that the last month or so of grief and sleepless nights had taken its toll, but instead of aging him, the lines gave his face character. The effect was devastating.

She sucked in a deep breath and prayed for the strength to survive the coming months. "Yes, well, mealtime might be easier if you asserted some authority instead of allowing Alix to manipulate you." She tempered the lecture with a smile and a laugh of her own. After all, she'd done her own share of allowing the little girl to have her way. Looking at that lopsided grin and mop of curls, Chelsie could almost see her sister. She lost her heart every time.

"Manipulate? I don't"—he shook his head—"yes, I do. But I pay for it, believe me. My clothes were covered with food."

She chuckled. "Might be easier, not to mention cleaner, to feed her with nothing on." A flush heated her cheeks and she rolled her eyes in embarrassment. "I can't believe I said that."

"Neither can I, but I'll take it under advisement."

Having already let her mind wander in that direction, visions of him naked came much faster this time. She was certain he'd be magnificent nude, and just as certain she had no intention of finding out.

These wayward thoughts didn't bode well for her handling of their time together. She needed to gain some control herself. "Sorry. I tend to speak my mind." She shrugged, determined to forge ahead, regardless of her big mouth.

"I noticed." He smiled again. "Mind if I join you?" He gestured to the beige couch and nodded, sliding her folder onto the stone cocktail table before her.

"What made you change your mind?" His penetrating gaze assessed her, and she struggled not to fidget under his scrutiny. After all, she'd set herself up for this and had to see it through.

"You didn't just drop in for the hell of it," he said, suddenly wary.

"No, but we do have to work out the details and you've just pinpointed one major flaw."

"What?"

"Your blatant and undisguised distrust of everything I do or say." She sighed and leaned on an armrest. "Look, I'm not asking for your complete faith. After that hearing, I understand your position. But this is your idea, so you must think I have some positive qualities or you wouldn't want me around Alix. Am I right so far?"

"So far you're on your way to one hell of an opening argument, counselor. Go on."

"All I'm asking is that you reserve judgment. Let my actions speak for themselves without your coloring them with preconceived notions that may or may not be correct." Chelsie grinned. "And for the record, they probably aren't."

"We'll see." His lips twitched as he tried to suppress a laugh, letting her know she'd made progress.

"Good. So for the duration, no more jumping to negative conclusions and unwarranted assumptions. Agreed?" she asked.

"Agreed. What else?"

"Watch it, counselor. I might begin to think you're easy."

His eyes focused on her lips. "As I said, we'll see."

Flustered by his double meaning and wanting what she could not let herself have, she rushed on. "I'll give you all my free time."

Pleased he'd made progress, Griff smiled. "And we appreciate it."

"Unfortunately, when you look at my days, that isn't saying much. There are a lot of times I won't be available."

Her words brought forth a well of disappointment so strong Griff was blindsided. "Those are the obligations you spoke of earlier?" She hadn't outright denied they were social in nature and she guessed that Griff couldn't help wondering about the extent of her involvement with other men.

"Yes."

"Whatever you can arrange with your schedule, I'd . . . we'd appreciate it. You've already seen what a difference you make."

"In the end, you might find that it's just coincidence."

He studied her intently. "I don't think so."

"I think you overestimate my capabilities, Griff. Alix reacted to an aunt she knows, but not as well as she knows you. I pay attention to her and she performs for me. Give her a chance and she'll be testing me just as much as she tests you."

"You seem very knowledgeable about children. Sure you haven't got one or two stashed away that no one knows about?"

Heavy silence descended upon him like fog. The flash of pain that crossed her features could only be described as grief. He should know. The first week after his brother's death, he steadfastly avoided the bathroom mirror. He hadn't bothered to shave until Ryan made a poor joke about his appearance frightening Alix.

Griff glanced again at Chelsie. With her arms

wrapped around her body, she reminded him of a
lost child. He was struck by the urge to enfold her
in his arms and chase away her unknown demons.
Based on their previous encounters, his abrupt ending to their kiss included, he doubted she'd let him
near. And, he reminded himself, he shouldn't want
to try.

She sucked in a shaky breath and plastered a fake
smile on her face. Her valiant effort to compose herself pierced his heart. His intended joke had obviously hit a very tender nerve.

"No children in the closet," she joked. "Just some
family skeletons."

"Glad to hear it. Now, what type of schedule did
you have in mind?"

She jumped at the new topic, animation sparking
her voice. But he didn't have to dig deep to notice
pain still lurked in the depths of her eyes. "I could
come by for supper sometime. That is, if the offer's
still open."

"It is. What about your caseload?"

"I'll take one day at a time. If things become un-
manageable . . ."

"Let me know. We'll work something out. You're
referring more cases than you'd like and I'm building a practice. I think we could help each other."

She cocked her head to one side. "Really? You
aren't even sure you like me."

If you only knew. His mind reminded him of how
little time she had spent with Alix in the past, of the
custody case and her initial rejection of his plea for
help. Yet no matter how strong his distrust, he
sensed there was much more to Chelsie Russell than
he'd seen so far. His body certainly wanted to know

her better, and their time together would be a trial in the truest sense of the word.

Being close to Chelsie and not allowing desire to flare between them wouldn't be easy. If he were smart, he'd make sure they spent only necessary time together, the hours needed for Alix's well being and nothing more. So why did he find himself pushing for more than she wanted to give? Not a smart move, he silently cautioned. Especially because where she was concerned, he had no intention of giving in return.

So why had he even mentioned a business arrangement?

"Don't rush into anything you'll regret," she cautioned, echoing his silent sentiments. "It's one thing to have me around for an hour or so a day. Working together is a whole different story. This arrangement is meant to help Alix. It's temporary."

He knew that. He'd planned things that way. So why did her pragmatic insistence on a short-term arrangement bother him?

"Which brings me to my next point."

"Anyone ever tell you you're long winded?"

She grinned. "Every judge in family court."

"I thought so."

"Those obligations keep me busy two nights a week and some weekends." She paused, obviously deliberating how much to tell him. "I volunteer at a women's shelter downtown."

He'd been expecting something more personal than volunteer work. Something akin to a jealous lover. Relief overwhelmed him, followed by frustration. What she did with her free time was none of his concern. He knew better than to care. He admired her dedication, but wondered at her initial reticence to discuss the subject. Helping others was nothing to be ashamed of, and it enabled him to rethink his opinion of her selfish nature.

Griff did not want another reason to like Chelsie or want her around. He cleared his throat. "I have no intention of interfering with your life. I appreciate the help, however much or little you can give. Your tour of duty will be over before you know it," he said, forcing a laugh.

She didn't laugh with him, testament to how difficult this entire situation had become for both of them.

"Before we make this definite, think about what you're asking," she said. "What happens when you decide Alix is doing well enough that you can throw me out of her life *again?*" she asked.

He winced at the blunt way she'd phrased her thoughts. Had he been that callous with her? Of course he had. "You're her aunt. Why don't we take things one day at a time, as you said?"

Chelsie shook her head. "She's a child. One who's lost both parents," she said gently. "You can't toss people in and out of her life and expect her to adjust."

Again he'd underestimated her. When Chelsie cared, she cared deeply. No one had ever focused that sort of emotional attention on him, and Griff had little time or understanding for deep-seated affection. Ryan's constant friendship and, until recently, Griff's relationship with his brother's family were the only exceptions. Thanks to his guardianship of Alix, he'd been thrown into the fire, but it was impossible not to give back to a little girl who gave everything and needed even more. But children were different, unjaded—until they grew up and learned to manipulate.

But here was Chelsie, fighting for her sister's child, showing love Griff hadn't even known she had in her. Glancing over, he wondered how it would feel to be the recipient of such unconditional love. *Wonder all you want, buddy. You'll never know.* He'd been trampled on twice. Only a fool set himself up for a third time.

Still, he admired Chelsie's foresight. He had only thought as far as bringing her into their lives, not edging her out. For some reason, he didn't want to dwell on the end of a relationship they hadn't even begun. "We'll work things out," he heard himself say. He had no idea how.

She leaned forward, gesturing with her hands as she spoke. "People aren't made of stone, *counselor.* They can't suffer loss upon loss and be expected to cope. You can't dictate how they live their lives." She sat back against the couch and crossed her arms over her chest.

He narrowed his eyes. Just who was she talking about? Alix, obviously. He already sensed her innate feelings for the little girl, and he wouldn't deny Chelsie visits. Surely she knew that.

That left Chelsie herself. Without a better road map to her feelings, he couldn't figure out where to go from here. "Just what do you want me to say?" he asked.

"If I'm going to have any part in this, I need to know I'll have a say in how things end. That when I stop coming by on an almost daily basis, she won't think she's been abandoned again." Her voice cracked under the strain of her emotions.

From the determined look on her face, Griff knew unless he came up with a satisfactory answer, she'd walk out and find a way to see her niece on her own. But he found himself at a loss.

Was he prepared to give her a role in deciding what was best for Alix? That necessitated a leap of faith in Chelsie he wasn't sure he was prepared to make. He'd just lost an internal struggle and accepted the notion that he needed her help, accepted her presence in their lives, if not his strong desire to know her better.

She claimed to want a say in when and how they parted. An innocuous idea, in and of itself. But what if he wanted to end their arrangement before she felt it was time? Worse, what if he and Alix weren't ready when Chelsie decided to call it quits? His mother had walked out. So had Deidre.

He looked at the woman sitting across from him, her angular jaw set, her fists clenched, and her dark eyes full of emotion. She already affected him on too many levels. Could he give her the power to hurt him as well?

Alix cried out in her sleep. Griff jumped to his feet, but she'd quieted again. He'd need to check on her in a minute.

"Well?" Chelsie asked.

Leaning against the mantel for support, he focused on the ever-present picture of Jared. *Help me out here, little brother.* No response came.

Griff thought of his niece. Did Chelsie's ability to hurt him really matter in the scheme of things? Hell, yes. Did he have a choice? Absolutely not.

He looked at Chelsie. "There's no need for you to contemplate walking out of Alix's life. You'll always be important to her, her one link to her mother. You'll get a vote in how things go," he said with more certainty than he felt.

He'd given her more than she asked for. Once the decision had been made, he couldn't seem to help himself. Her emotions, which always seemed to bubble at the surface and which she did little to hide, affected him in myriad ways, none of which he understood.

"Thank you." Her eyes misted, sparkling with unshed tears.

"You're welcome." Griff sensed her reaction went beyond gratitude. He'd missed an important clue, a key to understanding Chelsie better. But he wasn't about to push. Alix needed him and they'd covered enough ground for one night. There would be plenty more.

"I knew you'd see how important it is for Alix that we end this family-like scenario correctly when the time comes. We'll work it out. After all, we're doing this for her, remember?"

Mrs. Baxter finished the last of her dinner and placed her napkin on the table. "This is the first night Mr. Stuart hasn't made it home for dinner since I started working here."

Chelsie smiled. "That's because his practice is picking up. There's not a lawyer alive who doesn't understand the meaning of long hours. Don't throw your food, sweety." She bent to retrieve the vegetables Alix had not so subtly dropped on the floor.

"Well, I'm sure he feels more comfortable staying out knowing you're here."

"I'm sure he does."

Griff probably welcomed the reprieve from the polite formality of the last few evenings. *Please pass the salt. Thanks.* Silence. *Please pass the potatoes. Thank you.* More silence. *Dessert? None for me, thanks.* Chelsie nearly cringed at the memory. Only Alix had rescued them from freezing around each other completely.

"Since you've agreed to come by, he's much more relaxed. Even Alix senses the change."

Chelsie arched an eyebrow. Had the older woman slept through the last few evenings? "Relaxed is hardly the word I'd use." Chelsie redirected Alix's spoon away from her hair.

"I'm not talking about the Cold War you two have set up." Mrs. Baxter chuckled. "Tension's been so thick you could cut it with a butter knife." She patted Chelsie's hand. "You'll get used to each other. This arrangement's a blessing."

"You mean you don't mind? I was concerned you'd feel slighted."

"By you? You're her aunt, for goodness sake. Besides, before I took this job, I suggested to Mr. Stuart that he might want to hire someone younger for this position. Cooking, cleaning, keeping up with a two year old. Whew," she said, wiping a hand over her brow.

Chelsie laughed, but she knew the woman's gray hair was an illusion and that she had both the stamina and the desire to care for the little girl. "What did he say?"

"That he didn't need some young girl practicing

at playing mommy. Asked me if I could handle the job, and when I agreed, he hired me. But I don't mind telling you, the days are long."

"How have the nights been this past week?" Chelsie knew her scheduled time with the little girl, as well as with Griff, hinged upon Alix's moods and sleeping patterns.

"After the day I put in, I pretty much sleep like the dead. Mr. Stuart says they're still the same. But Alix isn't. She's a happier child."

"I'm glad for that, but time works miracles. Like I told Griff, you might find her emotional recovery and my presence are just coincidence."

She shook her head. "Nonsense. Anyway, you lighten my load, and that's a big help."

"Unfortunately, it's only temporary."

"We'll see." A kindly smile touched Mrs. Baxter's lips.

Chelsie ignored the comment. If the older woman held out any hopes of something permanent forming between her and Griff, she'd be disappointed. They could barely manage to relax enough to be in the same room. Not that Chelsie wasn't fully aware of him every moment they were together. She just wasn't fool enough to act on the attraction.

Chelsie reached for the dirty dishes.

"I can handle things in here," Mrs. Baxter said, taking the plate out of Chelsie's hands.

"Okay. I'll give little Miss Manners here a bath."

She scooped up the child and began the ritual that was now second nature. Funny how fast she'd fallen into the mommy role. The thought frightened her, because it was the very thing she'd promised herself would not happen.

Alix shrieked and smacked her chubby hands against the water, causing a small wave to cascade over the side of the tub and drench Chelsie's shirt. Chelsie pulled at the beige silk camisole and groaned. "Good going, squirt. Now I'll have to stop home before I go back to the office."

A last-minute hearing in the judge's chambers had delayed her, so she'd had no time to go home and change clothing. She glanced down and frowned. Obviously, taking off her suit jacket hadn't been the way to avoid getting soaked. That she couldn't stay one step ahead of a two year old was more embarrassing than she cared to admit.

The little girl laughed and splashed again. Chelsie chuckled and resigned herself to another long night. Griff might hope to gain sleep from this arrangement, but Chelsie certainly could not. Between her heavy caseload, her volunteer work at the shelter, and her hours with the Stuarts, she had little if any time left for sleep.

Despite all the pain that could result from this arrangement, she wouldn't give up one second of her time with Alix. Chelsie knelt over the edge of the bath tub and attempted to rinse shampoo out of the squirming child's hair.

Alix splashed again. Chelsie laughed and splashed back. Why not? Her shirt was already saturated and the little girl loved the water play. After exhausting both herself and Alix, Chelsie attempted to pull her out of the tub, though by the child's screams of protest, Chelsie was the only one worn out.

"Mrs. Baxter had the right idea. Maybe I should have volunteered for dish-washing detail," she murmured.

"And here I thought bath time was the highlight of your evening."

Chelsie whipped around, startled by the sound of Griff's voice. Her heart fell into a steady staccato rhythm. "I thought you wouldn't be home until late."

"And miss spending time with my favorite girl?" The reference definitely referred to Alix, but his gaze lingered on Chelsie much longer than necessary.

His eyes smoldered, heating her body with a glance. No one, including her ex-husband, had ever looked at her quite that way before. She relished the feeling.

Chelsie thought she had given up on romantic fantasies long ago. The first time her husband had hit her, he'd attributed it to a stressful day at work. She'd accepted his apology.

The second time he'd displayed his temper had been over a burned meal. Though she hadn't understood, she'd believed his promise of nevermore. But she'd never looked at him the same way again.

And he'd never gazed at her as if nothing else in the world mattered. Not in the beginning and certainly not after . . . in her mind, she saw herself teetering in shock, a large shadow looming over her.

She shuddered at the dark memories she thought she'd banished from her waking hours.

"Hey, you okay? Chelsie!"

Griff's deep familiar voice rescued her from the past. With a gentleness she'd only seen him use on Alix, he brushed her damp bangs out of her eyes.

"You okay?" he asked again, as his fingers trailed down her cheek, lingering for a moment before he pulled back.

"I'm fine." Her voice quavered, an embarrassing reaction to his caress.

"Forgive me for saying this, but you don't look fine." The concern in those hazel-colored eyes touched a place deep inside her. When he dropped his defenses, she felt transported back to the days before her naive belief in happily ever after had been shattered.

"Exhaustion," she said with a forced smile. "Every once in a while, my schedule catches up with me. I'm okay. You've got enough to worry about without adding this stray to your list."

She swallowed hard, determined to ignore Griff's furrowed brows and blatant look of disbelief. But the masculine scent of his cologne made ignoring him impossible. The woodsy fragrance heightened her senses. His mere presence obliterated her memory until she almost believed the past didn't matter. *But it did.* There wasn't a man out there who'd think otherwise, Griffin Stuart included. Alix was his niece, not his flesh and blood. He would want his own children. Though Chelsie could offer many things, she could never give him that.

Flustered, she glanced down and busied herself closing the baby shampoo and wrestling a rubber duck out of Alix's playful hands.

"You sure you're okay?" he asked.

"Absolutely." She'd survived the past five years by making the best of whatever life brought her way. No sense in changing things now. Moments like this were rare. She ought to cherish them. Heaven knew, she wouldn't have many more in her life.

Ignoring Alix's thrashing, Chelsie scooped her up and out of the tub, wrapping her in a large bath towel. "Someone looks like a prune," Chelsie said, tickling the little girl and drying her off at the same time.

"Why don't I take over? I'm sure she's worn you out by now."

"She's a handful, that's for sure."

Alix greeted that pronouncement with a giggle and an aborted attempt to dive back into the tub.

"Proof that not only do children understand everything, they live up to our expectations," Chelsie murmured.

"Amen. Must have learned those tricks from her daddy. Jared knew how to con me into letting him do just about anything."

Chelsie smiled, grateful that he'd spoken of his brother with fondness and not despair. Griff had devoted his life to Alix, but deserved to move beyond the boundaries imposed by his grief.

"Sounds like you were the typical big brother."

"More like the typical father."

"Really?"

He nodded. "But now's not the time to get into those stories. Wouldn't want to bore you," he said. "Pajamas and bedtime, squirt."

Alix ran for her bedroom, losing the towel halfway down the hall. Griff followed, his deep laugh resonating as he walked.

Chelsie drained the water from the tub and wiped her hands on a towel. She knew for certain she wouldn't be bored. She couldn't help but be curious about Griff's long-standing relationships, Jared and Ryan included. Along with his commitment to Alix, they showed his ability to sustain healthy friendships and maintain emotional bonds, something she hadn't encountered in a man before.

But she also understood the importance of respecting a person's private space. By acknowledging Griff's right to privacy, she hoped to ensure her own. Chelsie shut off the bathroom light. If she were smart, she'd join Mrs. Baxter downstairs.

With a knowing sigh, she turned and walked toward Alix's room. Her brain cells must be in short supply this evening. Watching Alix snuggle against Griff as he tucked her into bed was definitely a stupid move, one she'd promised herself not to repeat.

FIVE

Chelsie didn't say a word. She didn't have to. The scent of lilacs permeated the air, making Griff painfully aware of her presence. He placed Alix in her crib and covered her with her favorite blanket.

"Puppy," she said, jumping up and demanding a white ball of fur that lay on the floor. Griff retrieved the stuffed animal and coaxed Alix back into the crib.

All the while, he sensed Chelsie's intense scrutiny.

He drew himself up and leaned against the crib rail, glancing over his shoulder in the direction of the door. Chelsie met his gaze and a feeling of *déjà vu* crept over him. He found himself unable to look away. Like a recurring dream, he felt as if they were replaying her first night in the house. She drew a deep breath and exhaled, the action culminating in a soft sigh. Unwilling to let her see the effect she had on him, he turned toward his niece.

He bent over and kissed Alix good night, offering a silent prayer that for once she'd sleep without torment. He turned and walked toward the door where Chelsie waited, but she didn't notice him. Her pupils had dilated and she seemed distracted by her own thoughts.

He'd caught a glimpse of that shaken expression

before. Chelsie's lost-little-girl look hit him hard. Not for the first time, he questioned what painful memories drew her out of the present and into the past. At times like this, she looked like anyone but the strong attorney who fought for the rights of others. Who fought for Chelsie?

She met his gaze suddenly and turned away. Though Chelsie ignored him, he couldn't do the same. He'd noticed she still wore the wet silk tank that molded against her breasts. He nearly choked on a groan. Scanning the room, he reached for her jacket.

He touched her shoulder. Without a word, she turned to him. Tears not only shimmered in her dark eyes, but dripped down her face. He brushed her satiny skin with his thumb, catching the moisture before it fell.

If he leaned a fraction closer, she would be in his arms. He didn't think she would resist. She might even welcome the distraction from whatever haunted her. Though sex might be the answer to Griff's desires, it would do nothing to dispel Chelsie's pain. Fulfilling his needs would have to wait.

She gave him a shaky smile and wiped the droplets with the back of her hand. "I never react rationally when I'm overtired," she murmured.

Pretending to accept the explanation, he nodded and held out the suit jacket. She glanced down at her chest and then back at his face. He smiled, but his eyes didn't follow her gaze. He'd already memorized the sight of her pink nipples beneath the sheer silk.

She rotated and allowed him to help her into the jacket. She'd met his grin with dignity. Though she flushed crimson, she remained silent. He placed a hand on the small of her back and led her out of the room, shutting the door lightly behind them.

"Thank you," she whispered.

He smiled. "No problem."

They stood in silence.

"I'm sure you've got plenty of work waiting at the office," he finally said.

"More than you can imagine."

"I'll let you get to it, then."

She nodded, but didn't make a move to leave.

"I'm sorry I was late. I certainly didn't mean to hold you up."

Chelsie shrugged and fiddled with the buttons on her lapel. "I'm here for Alix."

Not you. The unspoken words lingered in the air. He didn't believe her, and the realization startled him. As an attorney, he recognized the many ways open to a client determined not only to withhold information, but to remain detached from the surrounding proceedings.

Chelsie exhibited classic symptoms. She couldn't meet his gaze. She fiddled with unimportant tasks and any object in the vicinity of her hands. She reiterated her point *ad nauseam. It's a temporary arrangement. I'm here for Alix. We're here for our niece.* How many times would she repeat the refrain? As many as it took for her to believe the words herself.

Just a week ago, Griff would have used her own defenses against her, jumping on his belief in her eagerness to end the arrangement and abandon them both before Alix was ready.

Now he saw all too clearly that Chelsie fought her own inner battles that had nothing to do with him. Did that mean he had forgiven her past mistakes? Decided she had nothing in common with Deidre and his mother? On those points, he'd reserve judgment.

She closed the last button on her suit, hiding all evidence of the beautiful body beneath. "I'll see you tomorrow?"

He nodded.

She walked away, then stopped to glance back at him. "Tomorrow's no good. It's my sleep-over night at the shelter."

He clamped down on his disappointment. "The next day, then."

She nodded and rushed down the hall.

Griff leaned against the wall and groaned. Bad enough the sexual attraction grew with each passing day. But did Chelsie Russell have to tug at his already battered heart? He hadn't a clue how to kill his growing feelings. Worse, he wasn't sure he wanted to.

Griff eased himself into the worn booth at the diner. "Sorry I'm late. A client wouldn't take no for an answer."

Ryan shrugged. "Refill. Coffee, black," he reminded the passing waitress. "And a BLT."

The woman looked at Griff. He glanced at his watch and shook his head, so she placed her pad in her apron and moved on.

Food would have to wait. "I'm already half an hour late to put Alix into bed and I still have a quick meeting with a client." He and Ryan always met on Wednesday nights, but since Griff had started his own practice, Ryan had grown used to Griff's no-shows. "You look exhausted. An all nighter?"

"I spent last night staked out in front of some dive in the 'Combat Zone'," Ryan said.

"Boston's answer to sleaze. What were you doing in a red-light district?"

"Domestic dispute."

"I thought you didn't take those kind of cases anymore. Breaking up marriages made you sick, or some such nonsense." Griff snorted. "If you ask me, anyone who hires you for a case like that is halfway to a divorce already."

Ryan shook his head. "Still cynical as ever, I see."

"Like I don't have a reason," Griff muttered.

Ryan cocked an eyebrow. "Back to the all-women-are-alike mentality?" he asked.

"Aren't they?"

"I don't know. Was your sister-in-law anything like Deidre?"

That gave him pause. In truth, he'd always liked his brother's wife. Never once during the frequent family dinners and nights he'd shown up unannounced had he ever sensed a similarity between his aloof fiancée and the warm, loving woman his brother had married. Nor had he seen a comparison to his mother, who'd earned the name only by giving birth to two children.

"No," he reluctantly admitted. "Shannon was unique."

"She was special, but not unique. Exceptions to every rule," his friend said with a smug grin.

Were there? Griff couldn't help thinking of Chelsie. She was Shannon's sister, and blood counted for something. If the past few weeks were any indication, Chelsie might well be more like her sister than like her wealthy, selfish parents.

Time would tell.

"Maybe you just haven't found the exception of your own," Ryan suggested.

Maybe he had and wasn't ready to accept it. "Don't you ever get tired of spouting advice?" Griff asked. "Maybe if you didn't spend every night on surveillance, you'd have a life of your own and could quit worrying about mine."

Ryan didn't answer, a rarity in and of itself.

"So what were you doing last night, anyway?" Griff asked.

"Family favor."

"Your sister?"

"Yeah. For once, I didn't mind the boredom. I came up empty." He formed a zero with this thumb and forefinger.

"Guess she appreciates you more now than when we used to tag along after her," Griff said. "Even Jared grew up to appreciate his pain-in-the-butt older brother."

"Yeah. After he got over the fact that we tailed him home from school to protect him and ended up blowing his first chance at scoring with the woman of his dreams," Ryan said on a laugh.

With his little brother gone, the times when Griff, Ryan, and Jared had stuck together through school, sweat-filled summers on the streets, and a rough neighborhood seemed like a distant memory. But to Griff's surprise, Ryan's recollection made him smile instead of gripping him with grief.

There were moments, Griff was sure, when his little brother had resented Griff and Ryan's constant interference, but all three of them had benefited from the closeness they'd shared.

"So how's the squirt?" Ryan asked, changing the subject.

Griff leaned back against the plastic seat cushion. The diner across from the local courthouse wasn't known for comfort or good food, just quick service. "Actually, Alix is great."

"Sleeping?"

"Not through the night, but for longer hours at a stretch." Coincidence or not, Griff appreciated the pre-bedtime hours Chelsie gave to his niece. She might not have children of her own, but the woman definitely had mother potential. Some man would be lucky to get her.

"What's with the scowl?" Ryan asked.

"Nothing."

"So what do you think made the difference?"

Griff had avoided this subject for the past two weeks. But Ryan had been a true friend when he needed one, so Griff decided to level with him and accept the consequences.

"I've got help."

"Anyone I know?"

"Chelsie Russell."

"Hot damn, I knew it." Ryan smacked his hand on the table. "I haven't heard from you in over a week, so I figured something was up." He paused to gulp the remainder of his coffee. "Well, I hope things work out for you."

"That's it?"

Ryan placed a hand over his heart. "You wound me. I'm a sensitive guy. I know when to keep my mouth shut."

"You're a pal." Griff stood. "I've got to get back."

"Listen, if things are serious, I could do a little digging. See what turns up."

"No!"

"Touchy."

"I thought you were sure Chelsie was my answer to life," Griff said, shooting Ryan a questioning look.

"That was before you went and got yourself hooked. Now it's my duty to watch out for you."

Griff rolled his eyes but didn't bother to dispute his friend. Old habits didn't die, even when they were no longer necessary. Not to mention that arguing with Ryan was never a worthwhile pursuit.

"Don't do me any favors," Griff said. "Just leave things alone." Chelsie's business was her own. As long as she looked out for Alix's welfare, Griff had no problems. He'd deal with his personal life himself.

"Anything you say." Ryan finished his coffee and stood. "Call me if you need anything."

"I will." Griff turned to go. "Hey."

"Yeah?"

"Glad to hear about your sister."

Chelsie popped in a video for Alix and settled the little girl on her lap. Alix snuggled against her chest, obviously tired after a long day. Normally, Griff would already be home, and they'd spend this time together. Like a family, her heart said. She squeezed Alix tighter, causing the child to squeal in protest.

"Sorry," Chelsie murmured.

She shook her head to dispel any fantasies that might be brewing. She and Griff had merely agreed from the start that acclimating Alix to a routine would be the first step in helping the child. Nothing family motivated about that. Unfortunately, until

Griff's absence this evening, she hadn't realized how much she enjoyed his company.

She rubbed her eyes to alleviate their burning. That she spent more time with Griff and Alix each evening probably contributed to her backlog of work and complete lack of sleep. Still, she hadn't broken her self-imposed promise. She'd kept a careful distance between herself and Griff. Despite the attraction, which had grown from a spark of desire into a tangible entity all its own, she'd managed to rein in her own needs whenever he was around.

As she'd feared from the beginning, as far as Alix was concerned, Chelsie had already lost her heart. The best she could do was avoid emotionally dangerous situations. So she hadn't put Alix to bed.

She hoped that wasn't about to change. When Mrs. Baxter received an emergency phone call from her son, Chelsie saw no need to detain her. As soon as Griff returned, he would tuck Alix in and Chelsie would head back to the office.

She glanced at her watch and silently prayed he'd be home in time. She couldn't allow herself to get any more attached to either Griff or Alix. If she did, she'd open herself to hurt far greater than any her husband had inflicted. After that experience, she'd fought to regain both her pride and her inner spirit. She'd won.

She hated to think of the damage loving and losing a man like Griffin Stuart would cause, not to mention losing another child. She shuddered and buried her face in Alix's curls. *You're about to find out.* She'd begun to enjoy her time with Alix and Griff. Too much, because she knew each day brought her closer to the end.

She gnawed on her lower lip and checked her

watch again. "Ten more minutes till bedtime, squirt." Where was backup when she needed it?

Two weeks ago, Griff had shaken Chelsie's hand and this crazy arrangement had begun. Tonight, as he drove home from a long day in court and a last-minute meeting with a client, their arrangement didn't seem so unusual. Even if he hadn't admitted it to Ryan, he liked knowing she'd be waiting when he got home.

The evenings she volunteered at the shelter were the longest he'd known in a while. That included the all-nighters he'd put in with Alix. With Chelsie gone, he'd putter around the house, forcing himself to concentrate on work or searching for something interesting to occupy his time. Not a good sign for a man determined to remain detached, he thought wryly.

A loud crash of thunder followed by a streak of lightning shattered the night. Raindrops pelted his windshield. Though he had to squint, he made out a yellow sign ahead. A detour alerted him to change his usual route home. Heeding the sign, he switched directions, accepting that he'd be home even later than planned.

Why didn't he heed the warning signs that Chelsie gave out? No matter what chores they shared, no matter how much time they spent alone or together with Alix, she kept a careful distance between them, withholding a part of herself. Probably the most important part.

But he'd begun to care for her more than he should. And that made the wall she'd erected especially frustrating. Though Ryan's offer had been tempting, Griff's cynicism didn't entitle him to delve into a past Chelsie wasn't ready to reveal.

If he allowed himself to get involved, he'd leave himself open to heartache that surpassed any inflicted by his ex-fiancée. Deidre had wounded his pride. Chelsie had the ability to destroy his soul.

Griff knelt down beside Chelsie. In sleep, she appeared as much the innocent as his niece. Looks could be deceiving, and yet a deep desire brewed inside him. He wanted so badly to believe.

Hadn't Ryan offered him a way towards acceptance? With the cases Ryan took and the bad marriages he'd seen, he had as much reason to be cynical as Griff, yet he held out hope. He not only liked women, he trusted. So hadn't Ryan given Griff an opening? He need only give Chelsie a chance.

He glanced at the woman curled into his oversized chair. Dark shadows circled her eyes, shadows he could only attribute to his own selfish need to have her near. She provided invaluable assistance, but after the past two weeks, Mrs. Baxter could probably handle things. The thought lay like lead in his stomach, and not just because of Alix.

He could never explain to his niece why her aunt no longer spent each evening with them. Nor did he want to try. The child's face lit up each time the doorbell rang. He'd be a fool to take that sense of security from her now.

He needed to assure himself Chelsie wouldn't walk out of their lives. When she woke, they had important matters to discuss. He wasn't sure he was ready, but he had no other choice. Not if he didn't want to lose . . . what? A possible future? He shrugged. He had no idea.

"Chelsie." He whispered, hoping not to startle her. He'd already seen how she reacted when frightened, and he had no wish to put her through that again.

She didn't stir. Exhaustion had finally caught up with her. He brushed gently beneath her closed lids, tracing the slight shadows with the pad of his thumb. Her eyelids fluttered open and long lashes tickled his skin.

His gaze locked with hers. Seconds passed, with no sound but their own breathing. Griff had no desire to break the silken silence that surrounded them or the fragile trust they'd begun to share. The slightest noise would have shattered the peace, so he did the only thing he could.

He levered himself up to face her, his elbows resting on the arms of the chair. Their faces remained only inches apart. Her scent drifted around him. Slowly, so she would know exactly what he wanted and have ample time to resist, he lowered his lips to hers.

The first time, he'd been as shocked as she, but he knew they'd been building towards this moment ever since. He only hoped she felt the same.

He began with a gentle exploration of her soft mouth. When she didn't pull back, he cupped the back of her head with his hand, threading his fingers through the dark mass and pulling her closer. Not only didn't she resist, she fully participated. For Griff, distrust, grief, even the pain of the past, faded in importance. Nothing mattered except the woman in his arms. Stopping was the last thing on his mind.

Chelsie parted her lips in a faint sigh and welcomed him. His lips, warm and soft against hers, created a sense of belonging he'd never before experienced. As she pulled him closer, need pummeled at him from all sides. Apparently she felt the same. Once relaxed from sleep, her breathing came in shallow gasps. When she exhaled a soft but urgent moan, the knowledge that he wasn't alone fueled his desire.

With her moist lips caressing his, Griff was lost. Warmth, wet heat, and a deep caring consumed him . . . and confused him. He tried to push aside the doubts and concentrate on his desire and the need to possess her, but finally heeded his confusion.

He pulled back slowly and Chelsie followed his lead. She ran a trembling hand through her hair, a movement he stilled by lacing his fingers through hers. He needed the connection as much as he wanted to relax her.

He cleared his throat, wondering how to broach this subject after the intimacy they'd just shared. "We need to talk."

The corners of her mouth turned up in a smile. "I think we just expressed ourselves quite clearly without words."

He acknowledged her statement with a nod. "This isn't about that."

"Okay," she said, suddenly wary. "What then?"

He touched her face again. Before she could pull back, he stroked her cheek. "You're exhausted, and I'm the cause."

"You didn't force me into anything I didn't want to do. Anyway, my work and my life are cyclical. The hectic times will pass."

"Maybe. But what if I could guarantee that even the hectic times wouldn't be so bad?"

"Have you looked into a crystal ball, or are you planning on stealing my clients?" she asked with a grin.

"What if I said the latter?"

Curious now, she sat up straighter in her seat. "What are you getting at?"

"I'm proposing a way for you to continue to see Alix, to lighten your work load, and to take on more clients, all at the same time. You might even get some sleep out of the deal."

"Impossible."

"Nothing is impossible if you have an open mind. I'm proposing a partnership."

He forestalled her argument with a wave of his hand. "I know we got off to a rough beginning and I didn't make things easy on you."

"Thank you for admitting that."

"That's the least I could do. Alix needs the attention you're giving her. But I can see by the last two weeks alone that this addition to your schedule has been rough."

"Like I said, it'll pass."

"Maybe it doesn't have to. We can help each other here. This isn't just a selfish thing, though that's what this arrangement has been from the start."

"Don't be so hard on yourself," she chided. "But what did you have in mind?"

"You've already said you're referring more cases than you'd like. I need to build a client base. Working together, you no longer dole out cases to other attorneys and I start a solid practice."

"Sounds like you've thought this through."

"Truthfully, I haven't. But talking this out is as good a means as any for finding flaws."

"What if we don't get along all that well? I'd call that a major flaw."

He glanced down at their hands, still intertwined. His thumb created circles on her soft skin. "After what just happened, I'd have to dispute that statement, counselor." He reached out and brushed a strand of hair off her cheek. He let the slight tremor that shook her pass without comment.

"Do you make it a practice to mix business with pleasure?" she asked, slowly removing her hand from his.

He chuckled aloud. "No, but I am glad to know you'd label that kiss pleasure."

She groaned.

"Look, Chelsie, I work out of the house. I'm always around for Alix. This way, you would be too."

"Low, counselor. Even for you." She jumped out of the chair, nearly knocking him over in the process. "I'm not that child's mother. Installing me in this house as if I were is unfair to her."

"And to you?" he asked in a low voice.

She didn't answer.

He stood, ignoring the cramping in his legs from remaining in a crouched position for so long. When he turned, she stood facing the fireplace. He reached out a hand to grasp her upper arm. "Turn around and look at me."

She pivoted slowly, her reluctance evident in her stiffened muscles and the way she kept a definite distance between them.

He met her solemn brown eyes with a serious stare of his own. "I would never do anything to intentionally hurt you or your relationship with Alix."

She sighed. Her muscles relaxed enough so that he felt sure she was listening. He released his hold, but she didn't move away.

"I know that."

He regretted pushing for an answer without giving her time to think. Before she could say no, he rushed on. "I'll admit things between us are strained. But I'm also willing to admit something's brewing."

"Okay."

"It has to be easier to share ideas with someone than talking to the walls."

"Okay."

"And you've got the experience dealing with real people. Mine is with institutional clients. I could learn from you."

She tried unsuccessfully to suppress a grin. "Cut the humble act. From what I've heard around family court, you talk circles around the most seasoned pros. So you can dispense with the I-need-you routine."

"How about a plain I want you?"

Heat rose to her face, causing a pink flush to tinge her cheeks. But instead of backing off, her soft hands grasped his chin and turned him to face her. *"I said okay.* If you'd stop rambling long enough to hear me, you'd realize I gave in a long time ago." She laughed. "And to think you called *me* long-winded."

He relaxed, though he wasn't foolish enough to think all his problems had been solved. An uphill battle awaited him. His own roller-coaster emotions were not going to be easy to deal with. Neither, he suspected, was his new partner. "You won't be sorry," he said.

"That, counselor, remains to be seen." She grasped his outstretched hand. As her satiny skin brushed his calloused fingers, more than a business handshake passed between them. And he had the sinking feeling she'd be proven right.

SIX

"Did you weight these damned things with rocks?" Ryan dropped the large box onto the floor with a grunt.

Chelsie laughed. "You should have seen me in law school. My book bag outweighed me."

"That I can believe. Is that the last of them?"

"Yes, and I can't tell you how much I appreciate the help." She glanced at Ryan, wondering what kind of man Griff would choose as his closest friend. Dark hair ended the similarities between the men. Ryan had harder planes and angles to his face than Griff, but his loyalty to those he cared for appeared to run just as deep.

"Anytime. Griff always volunteers me for the jobs he can't handle."

"I was wondering . . ."

"Excuse me." The sound of another voice in the room startled her and ended her chance to learn more about the Stuart family. Just as well, she thought. Curiosity could only lead to more intimate knowledge and even stronger feelings.

She turned to see Griff watching them, a scowl etching his handsome face. Though he'd offered to help her move things from her office, Alix had come down with a cold and he didn't want to leave her. Ryan had shown up in his place.

"Like I said, he's the brains, I'm the muscle," Ryan said.

"I did go to law school, remember? I know what those books weigh. And," Griff said, looking his friend over, "you could use the workout."

Chelsie tried and failed to suppress a grin. "Oh, shut up, both of you." She shook her head. "Men."

"I'm out of here. Next time another job's too much for you, remember to call me." Ryan bounded down the stairs.

"He's a good friend," Chelsie said as she pushed up her sleeves so she could begin the arduous task of unpacking.

"Like a brother." Griff leaned against the wall and stared into the empty room. Chelsie winced at the word brother. But Griff seemed lost in thought, so she doubted he'd even noticed. "Ryan grew up next door to us. We've always been close. Even when Jared was alive, it was always the three of us."

She nodded. She and her sister had grown up much the same way. With two fairly disinterested parents, they'd had no one to rely on but each other. Maybe that was what made the break in their relationship so difficult to bear. Chelsie had looked out for her sister in her own way, but phone calls and occasional lunches were pathetic in retrospect and provided little consolation now. In seeking to protect herself from further loss, Chelsie had deprived herself of even more.

With such a close bond between the brothers, Griff's feelings of loss had to surpass her own.

"The day my mother ran off, Ryan told my Dad that we'd take care of Jared," Griff said at last.

Chelsie held her surprise in check. If she disturbed his train of thought, he might not reveal any more. Despite her earlier admonitions to herself about satisfying her curiosity, she wanted to know this man in all the ways that counted.

When he remained silent, she spoke softly. "How old were you?" she asked.

"Twelve."

Old enough to hurt, too young to comprehend. Her heart broke for the little boy who'd lost his mother and to this day probably didn't understand why. She doubted even an adult could understand that kind of desertion. Many people prayed for the gift of bearing a child. This woman had thrown that away. "What happened?"

"She wanted more of some things, fewer of others."

Chelsie's eyes narrowed. "What do you mean?"

"More expensive trinkets. More money. More men." His bitter, harsh laugh told her what he thought of that. "And fewer responsibilities. Fewer children, to be exact."

If Griff was cynical, she now had an inkling why. "Why are you telling me this now?" Even as she asked, she feared she already knew.

Did he regret their change of status? Perhaps he'd decided the woman who'd sued him for custody at the behest of her wealthy parents was not to be trusted. Maybe he realized he'd had a lapse in judgment, but no more.

If so, she'd let him out gracefully, no matter how much it hurt. She'd had more than her own share of doubts about the partnership. In this case, grasping what little life offered might turn out to be a huge mistake. She braced herself for his excuses, promised herself she wouldn't react, and mentally calculated whether she could get her office back from the tenant she had sublet it to.

"Today's Jared's birthday."

"Oh." She hadn't been prepared for the admission. Without thinking, she walked over and took his hand, hoping to convey her feelings and her strength. "I'm sorry. You should have told me. We could have done this another time."

He shrugged. "It'll keep my mind off things," he said in a gruff voice.

He didn't want her gone. Relief warred with hurt over his pain, but she'd give him the distraction he desired. "Okay, then. Let's get started."

She headed for the first box, but he didn't release his grasp and she found herself pulled against him. His arms came around her waist and she sucked in a deep breath of air. She tilted her head backwards to look at him.

Raw emotion etched his features. In his eyes, she saw pain so deep only someone who had been there could comprehend. But she also saw something more, something his body wouldn't let her mistake. He held her flush against him, his erection pressing intimately against her.

"Griff. We have to work together. This is a mistake."

He loosened his hold on her waist. "Then walk away."

She ought to. He didn't need her. He needed someone, anyone to chase away the pain and help him get through this day. She could be here for him now and he'd still leave her when he discovered the truth. *So, go.* But her feet wouldn't move.

Her hand raised, seemingly of its own free will, to trace the tiny scar at the corner of his left eye. Once she touched him, it became too late to turn back.

His lips brushed hers. Without warning, he groaned and deepened the kiss, thrusting his tongue into her eager mouth. When he pulled her waist against him, she backed into the wall. The movement anchored her, enabling her pelvis to rock in synchronization with the expert movement of his tongue.

She thought she heard herself whimper under the assault. If he ground himself against her again, she might do just that. He pried her shirt loose from her jeans and ran his hands along her midriff. His thumbs brushed her nipples, causing them to harden into tight peaks.

And then she heard it again. The small whimper that could have easily come from her, but hadn't. "Griff," she murmured against his lips.

He groaned in protest. "Don't stop now." But he raised his head to gaze at her.

"Alix, I think," she said, glancing in the direction of the sound.

The slight whimper turned into an angry cry.

"Oh, hell." Griff ran his fingers through his hair, looking about as pleased with the interruption as she felt.

"Mrs. Baxter . . ."

"Has taken a week off to be with her son. I told her I could handle it."

When her mind began to function, she might be

grateful for the intrusion. Right now, all she noticed was a keen sense of frustration, a sensation as alien to her as desire.

"I'll go," she offered.

"No," he said brusquely, taking two steps back. "You start working up here. I've got it."

She nodded. Her tongue swiped over her lips. She still tasted Griff. Hugging herself, she watched as he bounded down the stairs two at a time. His reluctance to end the kiss had resulted in his eagerness to get away.

She turned to unpack, ignoring her still throbbing body. She reached for another book. Griff shouted so loud she would have heard him yell without the monitor. She vaulted down the stairs and dashed towards Alix's bedroom.

"What is it?" Only grabbing onto the molding on the door frame slowed her run.

His eyes met hers. "She's burning up. Should we give her aspirin?"

"No!"

Griff looked startled at her sharp tone.

"Never give a child aspirin," she said in a calmer voice. Chelsie leaned over the crib where the little girl lay shaking and shivering, and pressed her hand against the child's forehead. Her skin felt hot as an iron. Glancing over her shoulder, Chelsie saw Griff pacing behind her. "Call her doctor and ask him whether we should meet him at his office or the hospital."

He bolted out of the room. Chelsie quickly stripped off the child's clothes and lifted Alix into her arms. "It'll be okay, sweety," Chelsie crooned in her ear during the short walk down the hall to the bathroom. "I'm here, and Uncle Griff's here. We'll take good care of you, I promise."

Alix whimpered and tried to thrash around, but Chelsie held her fast.

While waiting for Griff to return, she held Alix over one shoulder and reached for the still damp bath towel with the other. After laying the towel in the sink, she opened the medicine cabinet and hoped she'd find what she was looking for without having to search. Once she located the rubbing alcohol, she propped Alix up on the counter while saturating the towel in a combination of alcohol and cold water. She wrung out the rag and sat on the toilet, wiping the little girl down with the cool compress.

She would have liked to repeat the process but knew she had little time. Instead, she returned to Alix's room and had her dressed by the time Griff returned.

"What did the doctor say?"

"He'll meet us at the hospital."

"Okay. Let's go."

He wrinkled his nose. "What's that smell?"

"Rubbing alcohol. Reduces fever."

Within minutes, they had Alix in her car seat and were headed for the hospital. "Where did all this knowledge about children come from, anyway?" Griff asked, keeping his eye on the road.

Chelsie swallowed hard and thought quickly. "Working at the shelter," she explained. During her brief pregnancy, she had read all she could about infant and child care, waiting for the day she'd hold her own baby in her arms. No point in explaining that to Griff now.

"Oh."

She placed a hand on his arm. "She'll be fine. Lots of kids run high fevers with things as minor as an ear infection," she said for his benefit. He looked pale and shaken and about to fall apart. "I've seen things like this before." Whether or not Alix's illness was as simple as she'd laid out for Griff didn't matter. Keeping him calm did. She'd let herself fall apart later.

He turned and she met his intense stare. "Thanks."

She smiled in return. He lifted her hand, wrapping his fingers around hers. His touch formed a tangible bond between them, stronger than anything that had passed between them before.

They drove the rest of the trip in worried but comfortable silence. Only when they reached the hospital did she feel Griff reluctantly pry his hand from her own.

Chelsie glanced down at her watch. "What did the doctor say again?"

"That her fever had spiked, but it's down now. They're just monitoring her." Griff leaned his head against the wall. He closed his eyes and wished for privacy.

He wasn't pleased with the fact that he'd stood by helplessly and let Chelsie handle what should have been his responsibility. But the thought of losing Alix as surely as he'd lost everyone else in his life had immobilized him. Now, with the immediate crisis over, the cold fear that ripped at his gut had begun to recede.

Allowing Chelsie into his life would just add another woman to the list of those who'd deserted him in the end. Erecting barriers didn't come as easily as it had in the past. He supposed he had Chelsie to thank for that. "Why don't you go get some sleep?" he asked.

"I wouldn't leave you now."

Later, then? The clock on the wall ticked off another minute, the sound echoing in the small waiting room. He opened his eyes and focused on the stark beige walls, but refused to allow himself the pleasure and agony of glancing in her direction.

"Eleven o'clock," she murmured. She stood and paced the confines of the limited space, her actions making him increasingly aware of her presence and whereabouts. "Are you sure it's just the flu?" she asked.

"Yes."

"And they'll let her go home in a few hours if the fever stays down?"

"Yes."

"What if she wakes up and gets scared?"

He groaned. "Would you just relax? Go get a cup of coffee or something." He stood and stretched.

She shook her head.

"Go home, then. Or at least stop pacing like you were her mother. You're making me nervous."

"I'll go home when I'm good and ready. And if you don't want me acting like her mother, you shouldn't have placed me in this damned position to begin with." Her eyes flashed angry sparks, but her voice shook, as well.

Griff recognized the accompanying signs of hurt, too. Shame overwhelmed him, but once spoken, his words lay like a chasm between them.

"I warned you, but would you listen?" she asked.

"Chelsie." He placed a hand on her arm. She shrugged off his touch.

"Of course not. You know what's best. You know what everybody can handle." She snorted in disgust.

"Calm down." He tried soothing her with his voice. "I'm sorry. It's been a long night and I'm as edgy as you are. And I'm used to dealing with things alone."

"And you prefer it that way."

"Yes. No. I can't lose someone else." Not Alix or Chelsie, but he wouldn't admit as much aloud.

Her shoulders sagged as some of the anger seemed to seep out of her system. "It's okay. I understand."

"One of us should get some sleep. I'll take the night shift and I'll catch some shut-eye tomorrow when you take over." A strand of hair had fallen across her cheek. Suddenly needing human contact, needing Chelsie, he reached to brush it away.

"When I proposed this partnership, the idea was for you to get more sleep, not less," he said. "So go, okay?"

"Okay. Now's not the best time to hash this out anyway. We'll deal with things tomorrow."

His eyes narrowed. "What things?"

She slung her purse over her shoulder. "Things," she said in a low but determined voice. "At least we haven't finalized anything," she murmured. "I'll check Alix on my way out."

"Be my guest," he said to her retreating back. The swinging doors shuffled closed behind her. "But don't think you're walking out on this arrangement just because I lack tact and finesse." And the brains God gave to most men.

Maybe he had come down with the damned flu. Self-protection was one thing. Driving away the woman who had kept him sane was another. A damned stupid move. As soon as he got Alix home, he planned on rectifying his mistake.

Chelsie stomped around the office. If she'd unpacked, at least she'd have the satisfaction of tossing her things back into the boxes. Now, she took the only means available to release her frustration. She taped closed the one box she'd had time to open.

"What do you think you're doing?"

"Leaving," Chelsie said without turning to look at Griff. At times, he read her too easily. Now he'd see a woman with no intention of carrying out her threat. But her childish actions allowed her to vent anger she couldn't decide where to direct, and she needed the release.

"No, you're not." He sneezed.

"Bless you. Why shouldn't I?"

"Chelsie, I'm sorry. I was tired. Irritable. Worried about Alix."

"Right. So you turned on me, the person you'd kissed hours earlier. Says a lot about your character."

He had to suppress a grin. Her sarcasm gave him a foolish hope that she didn't really want to leave. "My character leaves a lot to be desired. My taste in partners does not. Come on, give a guy a break."

Her hands stilled on the box. "How's Alix?" she asked.

"Napping. Fever's gone. My guess is she'll be raring to go in about"—he glanced at his watch—"one hour."

"Then you go on and get some rest. I'll handle Alix."

He sneezed again. She looked at him in concern. "Feeling okay?" she asked.

"Just tired. So if you don't mind, I'll take you up on your offer." At least if she had to watch Alix, Griff could be sure she'd still be there when he woke.

"Go on." She prodded his back with her palm. "Despite that nasty temper of yours, I might have lunch made when you wake up."

"Is that your way of saying we're still partners?"

"It's my way of saying you might get another chance." Her lips twitched as she tried to suppress a smile. "Speaking of chances, is that your third or fourth?" she asked.

He opened his mouth to reply and she snapped his jaw shut with her hand. "Quit while you still have a partner, partner."

Her dark-eyed gaze settled on his, unnerving him.

"Go get some sleep," she said in a husky voice.

He let his finger trail over her moist lower lip before turning and doing as she suggested. He didn't trust himself not to touch further. At this point, a solitary nap was the safest place for him to be.

He awoke with a scratchy throat and a pounding headache. His skin hurt to the touch. He groaned, which only caused the first two symptoms to increase in severity. A hangover, which he hadn't had since his college days, would feel better than this.

Chelsie knocked.

"Come on in." He propped himself up higher in bed.

"You must have been exhausted, because you slept through lunch and dinner. I figured I'd wake you so you could at least have something to eat before I left."

"How's Alix?" he asked.

"What's wrong? You sound like a frog." She walked to the side of the bed and snapped on a table lamp, causing him to squint until his eyes adjusted to the light. "She's fine. She woke up, played all afternoon, watched a video or two, and went back in for the night."

He ran his fingers through his hair. "And I slept through all that?"

She nodded. "You look awful."

"Thank you. I can't remember the last time a woman's compliment turned my head like that."

"Be serious. Your eyes are glassy, your face is flushed. How do you feel?"

"As lousy as I apparently look."

"Where do you keep the aspirin around here?" Grateful that she seemed to be taking charge, he gave in to his aching muscles and leaned back onto the pillows. "Bathroom medicine cabinet. Through that door," he said, and pointed to the master bath.

"Someone should have told me that baby-sitter and nursemaid would be part of the partnership agreement. I would have upped my percentage." He was about to dispute that, then realized he couldn't. Apologizing seemed like the next best alternative. But she softened her words with a genuine smile before heading in the direction he'd indicated.

"You probably caught some form of what Alix had. Open up," she said, upon exiting the bathroom.

He complied and she cut off any answer by sticking a thermometer in his mouth. "Don't go anywhere. I'll be right back."

She left as briskly as she'd come, giving him only a brief moment to view her from behind. Her jeans fit like a coating of paint and those legs seemed to grow in length each time he looked. If he felt feverish before, he'd hate to view the thermometer now. He closed his eyes and settled in to wait.

"Open," she said a few minutes later.

"You sure you weren't a drill sergeant in another life?"

"Cute." She paused to read the thermometer and frowned. "You've got a fever, Griff." She handed him a glass of orange juice from the nightstand. "You stay put."

"And who takes care of Alix?"

"As if you didn't already know. It's Saturday night, so neither one of us has any pressing work engagements tomorrow. Give yourself twenty-four hours for the fever to break. By then, you'll be on your feet and Mrs. Baxter will be back first thing Monday morning."

"She's out till the following weekend."

Chelsie shook her head. "She called to check in. I told her what had happened and she'll be back."

"Good."

"But for the next twenty-four hours, you're stuck with me."

It was what he'd wanted all along, but her physical presence wasn't all he needed, and her no-nonsense attitude irritated the hell out of him. Never mind that he'd caused her to withdraw. He desired the woman who melted in his arms, not this wind-up nurse doll.

She grabbed the empty glass from his hands and her gaze raked him over from top to bottom.

"You're still in last night's clothes. Change and I'll make you something light for dinner." She turned towards the door. "I can last a measly twenty-four hours," she murmured.

He knew she hadn't intended for him to hear. "Chelsie?"

She glanced over her shoulder. He smiled as he devoured her with his eyes. "You're about to find out how long twenty-four hours can be."

Chelsie knew Griff's prediction of a long twenty-four hours had been said with the express intent of making her squirm. Despite his illness, the predatory look in his eyes accomplished his goal. However, he hadn't counted on his fever rising and his comfort level declining, making him ill equipped to do more than groan, complain, and drive her crazy. Amazingly, Alix slept on. After dinner, Griff, too, had fallen asleep.

By the time Chelsie had unpacked most of her office, cleaned up the kitchen, and finished the laundry she'd found piled in a heap on the floor, the clock read nearly midnight. After looking in on Alix, she decided to check Griff once more before collapsing on the couch in the den. They hadn't discussed sleeping arrangements, and Chelsie didn't feel right invading Mrs. Baxter's privacy by borrowing her bed.

With only the hall light to guide her, she tiptoed into Griff's bedroom. She stood at the foot of his bed and glanced down at his sleeping form. His bare chest rose and fell in steady intervals. She smiled, appreciating the changes wrought by sleep. With the tension gone, a carefree expression softened the lines in his face and relaxed his features. Even the razor stubble added a roguish charm.

A far cry from the withdrawn man she dealt with on a daily basis, this man represented pure danger. She wanted him as much as she needed to resist his magnetic pull. Resisting would be easy only as long as he slept on.

Turning her attention to herself, she realized she needed rest. Though she felt like a thief, she rummaged through his bureau drawers. She doubted Griff would appreciate being awakened while she asked if she could borrow a T-shirt.

She ducked into his bathroom and changed into the first shirt she'd found. After shutting the light, she padded through his bedroom. She heard his even breathing and knew he still slept. She couldn't resist one more look before she turned in for the night. Careful not to wake him, she sat on the edge of his mattress. In silence, she watched him sleep.

She understood his mercurial moods, understood his confusion and reluctance to turn their already precarious relationship into something deeper. His mother had deserted him in life, his brother in death. He acted like a man who wanted nothing to do with women and emotional commitment. One day his views would change. With the right woman, Griff would want to settle down and provide Alix with a full-time mother and little brothers or sisters.

When the time came, could Chelsie gracefully step aside? Could she maintain their partnership and watch him with another woman? Watch someone else take over the role she currently filled in Alix's life?

She'd always be the little girl's aunt, but Chelsie knew now that wouldn't be enough. A lump formed in her throat and she blinked, causing a tear to drip down her face. How had she let herself become so attached to either one of them?

Despite both of their reservations, they found themselves on the verge of a legal partnership and an emotional precipice. Who would catch her when she fell this time?

She sighed and reached over, brushing a dark lock of hair off his forehead. Nighttime always made her melancholy, and she chided herself for succumbing. Her own feelings didn't matter. For both Griff and Alix, Chelsie would do whatever was necessary, even at the expense of her own happiness. Right now, however, she needed sleep.

She braced her hand on the bed and started to rise. His hand on her wrist startled her, preventing her from leaving.

Chelsie sat back down, aware that she now shared a bed with an extremely sexy, awake man. "How are you feeling?" she asked.

"Better."

She narrowed her eyes. "Don't lie."

"Lousy."

"I'll get you more aspirin before I turn in."

"Where?" His question sounded more like a croak.

"On the den couch."

"Chelsie . . ."

"Be quiet, you'll hurt your throat. And don't make a big deal about it. I've slept on my own office couch plenty of times." She rose, eager to escape her desires. "I'll be right back."

She returned and watched to make sure he swallowed the tablets. Then he merely stared. Uncomfort-

able, Chelsie knew she ought to leave before she succumbed. "If you need anything, I'll be down the hall."

"Would you stay?"

The blunt question caught Chelsie by surprise.

"It's been a rough day or so with Alix," Griff explained. "On top of that, with Jared's birthday . . .
I need the company."

Somehow, Chelsie knew company was all he had
in mind—a friend for the dark times. Her heart
went out to him. She wasn't surprised. Over the
course of the last two days, she'd suspected the
worst. Falling in love wasn't supposed to be part of
her carefully planned future. And now that she had?
For Griff's sake more than her own, she'd have to
ignore the feelings.

"Please."

She forced a grin. "Okay. I guess sharing your bed
won't be such a big sacrifice."

"Thanks a lot."

He moved over and she lay down next to him. His
scent seduced her. The warmth of his body tanta-
lized her senses much the way his shirt caressed her
body. Both left her yearning for more. Darkness en-
veloped her and she blinked in an effort to orient
herself to her surroundings. With Griff lying so
close, she could barely think.

"Nice shirt," he said.

She groaned, causing him to chuckle.

"How come there are no men in your life?"

Her breathing stopped and she forced air into her
lungs. "I suppose you think lying here under the cover
of darkness entitles you to ask personal questions."

"No," he said, pausing as he spoke. "I think our
partnership, our friendship, and maybe something

more gives me the privilege of asking those questions."

She was well and truly caught. "Well, put like that, how can I refuse?"

His deep laughter warmed her. "That's the point. You can't."

SEVEN

Griff forced himself to wait for the tale of Chelsie's past and, hopefully, for something more. Her soft curves touched him lightly but enough to tease and entice.

"I was married once." The sound of her voice worked to arouse his curiosity more than anything else.

"And?"

He felt the rise and fall of her shoulders in a shrug. "It was short and more bitter than sweet. Happy now?"

Not yet. Griff edged closer, but to his chagrin, Chelsie lay on top of the covers, while he lay beneath. "Get up."

"And they say women are fickle," she muttered. She swung her legs off the bed and stood.

His eyes had adjusted to the darkness, enabling him to take in her slender form beneath his large white T-shirt. The material draped her breasts, the hem reached mid thigh, and her long legs were bare. His gut clenched with desire, yet right now, all he really wanted was companionship during another long, dark night.

Her move toward the door grounded his stray thoughts. "Where are you going?"

She raised and dropped her arms with a loud sigh. "Stay, Chelsie. Get up, Chelsie. What's next? Heel?"

He burst out laughing. He loved her sense of humor, even when she turned it on him.

Grasping the edge of the comforter, he turned it back, baring the empty side of the bed. "Surely you weren't warm enough on top of the blanket, and I couldn't get comfortable either."

"Oh." She eyed the space next to him.

"You can get back in now." He patted the sheet and grinned.

Hesitantly, she complied and settled in beside him. He glanced at the miles of linen separating them. "No one could accuse you of hogging the bed." She'd lain down, taking up only one quarter of the king-sized mattress. "I won't bite. I won't even try anything," he promised. "I just want to talk."

She maneuvered until she lay next to him. Her delicious scent might make that promise damned difficult, but he knew he would keep it. "Why was your marriage short?" he asked.

"I don't suppose I could change the subject?"

"Sure you could. But I'd just change it back."

She propped one arm beneath her head. "Okay. He wasn't the man I thought I'd married. He changed."

"And that hurt you."

She exhaled a harsh laugh. "In more ways than one."

"*He* hurt you?"

Her startled gasp revealed his guess had been correct. The anger fueled by that knowledge stunned him, as did the proprietary way he pulled her into his arms.

She tensed. With her back to him, he curled himself around her. When he did little more than smooth her hair and rest his chin in the crook of her neck, her muscles seemed to relax.

"What happened, Chelsie?" This time, he tensed, sure that as much as he'd wanted to hear the details of her past, he wouldn't like what he learned.

"I'd volunteered at a women's shelter in college and had seen too many women abused who then went back for more." She drew a deep breath, causing her body to quiver. "I never thought it would happen to me. For all my parents' faults—and they have many—they never raised a hand to each other or to us kids. I never thought I'd *allow* it to happen to me."

"You don't always know someone, even when you think you do." Thanks to his mother and ex-fiancée, Griff had discovered that himself, though not to the extreme Chelsie had.

"Shannon and Jared were lucky, don't you think?" Chelsie whispered the words.

He nodded in answer. Despite his poor track record with women, Griff envied his brother's ability to create a happy home with the woman he loved. For the first time in his life, he wondered if he was capable of the same, if a woman existed who would break down his notions and barriers and love just him.

He glanced down at Chelsie. Comfortable silence drifted around them. "What happened?" he prompted.

"We graduated from the same law school. He went

to work for a large firm, I worked for the D.A. He wanted money and power, I wanted to help others. Maybe that should have told me something."

"Come on. Lots of people have conflicting ideals and still make a marriage work. I'd hardly call that missing a sign of something serious."

"Maybe. Anyway, we were married for less than a year. With the hours first-year associates work, I rarely saw him. The few times he displayed his temper, I fell right into the trap. I accepted his apologies and believed he wouldn't do it again."

He sensed her anger at herself and at her ex.

"Obviously the marriage never got off to a strong start," she said. "One night, we went to a cocktail party at his law firm. One of the associates recognized me from my work at the local women's shelter. He'd been drinking and caused quite a scene. Blamed me for talking his wife into leaving him."

"Sounds like the guy was a real winner."

"Yes, well, when the shouting started, the senior partners weren't too pleased. Seems they were courting major clients at the time."

In what had to be an unconscious move, she curled into him. He wrapped his arms around her in a protective gesture, knowing as he held her that he never wanted to let go. Holding her tight, he mentally prepared himself for the untold part of the story. "And then?"

"My husband dragged me out of there. I thought he'd be disgusted with his associate and frustrated with the way the evening had turned out. Maybe he'd rant and rave a little, but a while had passed since he'd raised his hand, let alone his voice, so I figured that would be the end of it."

"I take it he said plenty?" And lashed out even more, Griff thought with dread.

"The elevator in our building had broken and I followed him up the stairs with him yelling the entire way—about how I caused that scene, how I should keep my nose out of other people's personal lives, how I should get myself a real job and start earning some money to help support us. You get the picture."

What Griff pictured was a spineless man too cowardly to stand up for his wife and too selfish to care. "And?" he asked softly.

"And he turned toward me to finish his tirade." Her voice quivered and her skin, which had been so soft against his, suddenly felt damp. At that moment, Griff knew he didn't want to hear any more. But Chelsie seemed lost in the past, as she had been so many times before. He shut his eyes to the darkness surrounding him, but he couldn't block out the truth.

"He grabbed my shoulders and shoved me against the railing. He wanted my promise that I'd quit, that I'd stop volunteering, that I'd do something with my life that he could be proud of instead of having to hide his head every time someone asked what kind of law his wife practiced."

Griff held her close, soothing her with gentle kisses against her neck, but she continued her story as if unaware of his touch. She began to tremble in his arms.

"My back was pressed against the metal railing and each time he shook me, my head hit the concrete wall. The first time, I was so stunned, I thought it was an accident. But he just shook me harder.

Each time, my head hit that damned wall. He had
a firm grip on my arms and I couldn't move. By the
time he stopped, I was dizzy. I couldn't catch my
balance. I think he knew that, but he released me
anyway." She sucked in a breath of air, as if needing
the fortification to continue.

Griff decided to spare her. "And you fell down
the stairs," he finished for her.

"When I came to, the paramedics were there.
They said, and this is a quote, 'Consider yourself
lucky you have a husband who cares.' "

They lay in silence. Soon, her trembling subsided
and she slept in his arms. He had more questions,
but none that mattered in the least. What she revealed had been bad enough. The details of what
happened after were unimportant. But the sudden
need to protect her signaled a serious problem.

He was beginning to care. Too much.

Chelsie awoke with a start. For a long while, she
lay in Griff's arms, savoring the feel of his body close
to hers. Last night's revelations came swarming back.
She'd only told that story once before, to the police.
At the time, she'd been so alone. In the aftermath
of what she'd come to think of as the main incident,
she'd never repeated the tale. Not to her parents,
who would hate the scandal should the episode be
revealed, and certainly not to her happily married
sister. She couldn't face Shannon with the shame of
what she'd allowed to happen, and later of what
she'd done.

The result had been a withdrawal of the only emotional support Chelsie had ever known. Once Shan-

non had gotten pregnant, the closeness they'd shared as siblings disintegrated even more.

To have Griff's unconditional support now meant a great deal. But then, Chelsie had omitted select details and he hadn't thought to ask. Her inability to have children and the way in which she'd dealt with her ex-husband would change his perception of her forever. Though she wouldn't have lied had he questioned her, she was grateful she had been spared the humiliation of admitting the truth.

Silence still reigned in the house. Maybe she could sneak out to the couch and avoid the agony of a pseudo-morning after.

She squirmed towards the edge of the bed. Griff locked one solid leg around hers, halting her effort.

"I won't pass judgment, you know," he said, obviously referring to her admission last night.

Chelsie closed her eyes. She'd been so close. "I never thought you would."

"Then why sneak out on me? It's not like we did anything and can't face each other in the morning. At least, not yet."

She rolled to face him and placed a hand on his forehead. "No fever."

"Yet." He smiled, a sexy grin she found impossible to resist. "Care to rectify things?" he asked.

Would she ever. Good thing reality prevented her from acting on her baser instincts. "Alix will be up soon."

"Have you looked at a clock?"

She shook her head.

"It's five in the morning. That means three things. One, Alix finally slept through the night. Two, with any luck, she'll continue her pattern of sleeping until six-thirty or so. Three, we have to celebrate number one." He raised himself up on one elbow and looked down at her. "Unless you have other plans, in which case you're free to leave."

His dark eyes simmered with a combination of amusement and banked desire.

Free to leave? Her heart already belonged to him and wouldn't allow her to walk away. She'd held her own feelings for this man in check for so long, she now wondered if he'd done the same.

She glanced over. "You're so kind, Griff. Always giving me a choice." She sighed. "Let's see. Should I stay or should I go?"

He chuckled. "What can I say? I'm a firm believer in free will." Clasping her hand in his, he brought it to rest against his cheek. "I care about you," he said in a more serious voice.

"More than you want to?"

"More than I should."

"So join the club." She laughed ruefully, understanding the full import of his words for them both. "How'd you get this?" She traced the corner of his eye with a fingertip.

He drew a deep breath, but remained still. "I jumped off a fire escape when I was twelve."

"Girl watching?" she asked with a grin.

He shook his head. "No, Jared watching. The kids at school heard about how our mother took off with a boyfriend. Jared would get into fights and the bigger kids would wait on the corner to finish the job."

"Protective older brother," she murmured, brushing his hair off his forehead.

"At least I had backup."

"Ryan?"

"Who else?" He stilled her hand midair, his fingers locking with hers. "It's not working."

"What isn't?"

"Distracting me. Changing the subject. But the choice is still yours."

He had to be joking. They'd already spent the night in his bed, awakened tangled together and half-dressed, and she'd bared her soul to the man she loved. Her choice? Not likely. The decision had been taken out of her hands long ago.

She recalled her philosophy and decided to grasp what life—or in this case—Griff offered. When she looked back on this time, at least she'd have a beautiful memory.

She gazed up at him, fearful all she felt would show in her face. But she wanted to be with him. At this moment, she couldn't recall a time when she hadn't. He'd pervaded every aspect of her life, including work, which had formerly been her escape. In so doing, he'd become an important part of her. Too important. But she couldn't worry about that now.

A passion simmered between them and now, no longer buried beneath the surface, it threatened to bubble over. And that was good, she thought, glancing into his desire-filled eyes. More than good.

"Okay, counselor," she murmured. "I choose you."

"Be sure." Griff could handle her changing her mind before they made love, but not tearful regrets and recriminations afterwards.

"I am."

He had to accept her word. Looking down at her tousled hair and barely parted lips, he could do nothing else. With one hand, he raised the hem of the shirt she'd borrowed and trailed his fingers along her abdomen. The silky texture of her skin jarred the rest of his body into a complete state of arousal.

She lay still, allowing his hand the freedom to wander at will. With his fingertips, he traced a line from mid-thigh along her narrow waist and over the curve of her breast. Pausing long enough to brush one hardened nipple with his thumb, he learned the feel of her skin. He inched his fingers downward.

She drew a shaky breath as her gaze fastened on his face. The trust he saw reflected in her brown eyes humbled him, especially after what he'd learned of her past. He wasn't sure he was worthy of that kind of faith. Though he'd do his best not to hurt her, he couldn't offer more than this.

Too much of himself had been torn apart, and the little that remained belonged to his niece. He could give Chelsie now. Perhaps that would be enough for her. He ignored the voice that asked if it would be enough for him.

"Griff?"

Looking at her curious expression, he realized that although his thoughts had rampaged out of control, his hand had stilled. "Sorry," he murmured and refocused his attention on what was important.

On Chelsie.

As he lowered his lips to meet hers, all hesitancy fled. Heat spread through him like a sudden burst of wind. The initial sensation stunned him, wreaking havoc with his body and soul.

Dipping his head, he caught her lips with his,

coaxing her with his mouth, his tongue . . . and a piece of his heart.

His hand, which had come to rest on her stomach, inched upward again. He tried to start slowly, to savor the feel of her beneath his touch, but she writhed beneath him, urging him to move higher and stroke faster.

He did, cupping her breast while brushing one sensitive nipple with his thumb until it hardened into a tight peak. All the while, he continued his gentle assault on her mouth, tasting her moist heat. When she moaned softly, he took the sound deep inside of him, into a place she'd already reached.

He wanted to feel her gentle hands, wanted her to learn the feel of him as he had her. What he needed, he realized, was to know she wanted him, too. The blood rushing through him, demanding an immediate response, attested to his desire.

Through the haze of need, he realized she hadn't done more than run her hands along his bare back. He lifted his head and drew a deep breath.

She gazed at him through passion-filled eyes. Though he liked what he saw, he wondered why she held back. "Touch me," he whispered.

Her eyes, which seemed heavy only seconds before, opened wide. He traced her moist lips with one finger. She opened her mouth to speak, then closed it again.

"What is it?" With his voice and movements, he attempted to strengthen the trust he had seen in her eyes.

"I don't know . . . I mean . . ." Her voice trailed off, her cheeks tinged pink in embarrassment.

She was wonderfully responsive, but hadn't initiated any physical contact. He suspected her marriage had taught her little about sex and even less about making love. Though he knew plenty about the act itself, he might know as little as Chelsie about the emotions involved. Until now, he hadn't cared enough to learn.

He reached for her hand and held on tight. "You don't have to know anything except what feels right for you."

"Teach me." Her words came out a combination of a plea and a dare. She probably didn't realize they'd be charting new territory together.

"Just feel," he whispered. With a gentle brush of his fingertips, he closed her eyelids. Long lashes fluttered against her cheeks.

"I want to know if your skin feels like silk." He let his fingers trail along her inner thigh, over the softness of her skin. Her muscles quivered enticingly beneath his touch, making his slow exploration even more difficult to maintain.

"I want to know if you taste sweet." He dipped his head and caught one nipple in his mouth. His tongue swirled around twice, before he tugged gently with his teeth. She whimpered with undisguised need.

"So," she said in a husky voice, "if I want to know exactly how much you want me, all I have to do . . ." Her seductive voice trailed off at the same moment her hand cupped him through his briefs.

He exhaled a slow groan, feeling desire swell and grow beneath her fingertips. "I should have known you'd be a quick student," he said on a ragged breath.

She chuckled, her eyes alight with laughter and a

sense of liberation and satisfaction he hadn't seen there before.

"Number one in my graduating class." As she spoke, her expression sobered, causing the light to dim. "But if this isn't what you bargained for, it's not too late to back out."

Her hand lay on his hard length, his body throbbed with unsatisfied need, yet she still offered him a way out. "What the hell was it like for you?" he asked, harsher than he intended.

"Short, quick, and to the point." Chelsie closed her eyes, her humiliation complete. *Not quite,* she reminded herself. Sex was another area in which she never quite managed to satisfy her husband. What she felt for Griff surpassed anything in previous experience, which would make disappointing him so much harder to bear.

"Never again," he murmured softly, brushing his lips with hers. As if keeping his promise, he seduced her with his mouth, his tongue darting in and out, feasting on her mouth with gentle but insistent determination.

His hands worked similar magic, seemingly everywhere at once. She didn't know which part of her body trembled. Her skin burned, yet she craved more of his touch. More of Griff.

She allowed him to carry her away, to a place where sensation ruled and rational thoughts were not permitted to intrude. This time, she participated, refusing to allow old insecurities and inhibitions to matter. After spending the night wrapped in his arms, separated only by a thin layer of cotton, Chelsie couldn't stand the wait.

She surprised him by removing his briefs herself,

then raised her arms and allowed him to slowly peel off her shirt. He paused to taste every inch of exposed skin, lingering over extra-sensitive areas until she begged him to hurry. He then removed her lace panties with the same exquisite care, tantalizing and teasing until she cried out his name and pulled him up for a long, hot kiss.

Griff settled himself between her thighs, the tip of his erection pressed against her in a definite promise of more to come. The emotional intimacy they'd shared surpassed the physical, stunning her, considering they hadn't yet made love. And though the notion frightened her, she wanted him too much to back out now.

"Chelsie?"

He raised himself up on his elbows, taking his upper body weight off her. Though she missed the feel of his warmth pressing against her breasts, her lower body was on fire. He pulsed against her, making her ache with need.

"Hmm?" she asked, barely capable of a coherent word, let alone a coherent thought.

"Protection. It's in the drawer."

"Don't need it," she murmured, out of her mind with wanting him, needing him inside her.

An instant later, he thrust into her, realizing her silent plea. For Chelsie, this might as well have been her first time. He filled more than a simple need. He filled her heart. She closed her eyes against the truth, but the tears she held back mocked her effort.

Before long, the feel of him gliding inside her had her writhing with the need for more. And then sensation took over, obliterating all thought except how right he felt inside her.

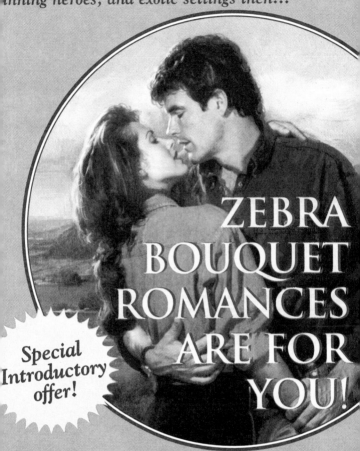

The publishers of Zebra Bouquet are making this special offer to lovers of contemporary romances to introduce this exciting new line of romance novels. Zebra's Bouquet Romances have been praised by critics and authors alike as being of the highest quality and best written romantic fiction available today.

Each full-length novel has been written by authors you know and love as well as by up-and-coming writers that you'll only find with Zebra Bouquet. We'll bring you the newest novels by world famous authors like Vanessa Grant, Judy Gill, Ann Josephson and award winning Suzanne Barrett and Leigh Greenwood to name just a few. Zebra Bouquet's editors have selected only the very best and highest quality for publication under the Bouquet banner.

You'll be treated to glamorous settings from Carnavale in Rio, the moneyed high-powered offices of New York's Wall Street, the rugged north coast of British Columbia, the mountains of North Carolina, all the way to the bull rings of Spain. Bouquet Romances use these settings to spin tales of star-crossed lovers caught in "nail biting" dilemmas that are sure to captivate you. These stories will keep you on the edge of your seat to the very happy end.

4 FREE NOVELS
As a way to introduce you to these terrific romances, the publishers of Bouquet are offering Zebra Romance readers Four Free Bouquet novels. They are yours for the asking with no obligation to buy a single book. Read them at your leisure. We are sure that after you've read these introductory books you'll want more! (If you do not wish to receive any further Bouquet novels, simply write "cancel" on the invoice and return to us within 10 days.)

SAVE 20% WITH HOME DELIVERY
Each month you'll receive four just published Bouquet Romances. We'll ship them to you as soon as they are printed (you may even get them before the bookstores). You'll have 10 days to preview these exciting novels for Free. If you decide to keep them, you'll be billed the special preferred home subscription price of just $3.20 per book; a total of just $12.80 — that's a savings of 20% off the publishers price. If for any reason you are not satisfied simply return the novels for full credit, no questions asked. You'll never have to purchase a minimum number of books and you may cancel your subscription at any time.

GET STARTED TODAY –
NO RISK AND NO OBLIGATION

To get your introductory gift of 4 Free Bouquet Romances fill out and mail the enclosed Free Book Certificate today. We'll ship your free selections as soon as we receive this information. Remember that you are under no obligation. This is a risk free offer from the publishers of Zebra Bouquet Romances.

FREE BOOK CERTIFICATE

Yes! I would like to take you up on your offer. Please send me 4 Free Bouquet Romance Novels as my introductory gift. I understand that unless I tell you otherwise, I will then receive the 4 newest Bouquet novels to preview each month Free for 10 days. If I decide to keep them I'll pay the preferred home subscriber's price of just $3.20 each (a total of only $12.80) plus $1.50 for shipping and handling. That's a 20% savings off the publisher's price. I understand that I may return any shipment for full credit no questions asked and I may cancel this subscription at any time with no obligation. Regardless of what I decide to do, the 4 Free introductory novels are mine to keep as Bouquet's gift.

Name _____

Address _____ Apt. _____

City _____ State ____ Zip _____

Telephone ( ) _____

Signature _____ BN07B9
(If under 18, parent or guardian must sign.)

For your convenience you may charge your shipments automatically to a Visa or MasterCard so you'll never have to worry about late payments and missing shipments. If you return any shipment we'll credit your account.

Yes, charge my credit card for my "Bouquet Romance" shipments until I tell you otherwise.
☐ Visa ☐ MasterCard
Account Number _____
Expiration Date _____
Signature _____
Orders subject to acceptance by Zebra Home Subscription Service. Terms and Prices subject to change.

BOUQUET ROMANCE
120 Brighton Road
P.O. BOX 5214
Clifton, New Jersey 07015-5214

Griff felt her quiver around him, felt her climb towards completion. He opened his eyes to watch her glistening face as she spiraled into a world that only he could share.

And he did, knowing the entire time that life after Chelsie would be drastically different than the life he had known before. His climax came with hers, unbelievably shattering in intensity. Unbelievably right.

He held her in his arms afterwards and felt her trembling. He remained silent. Words seemed inadequate. She'd been married and divorced; he'd been with his own share of women, a fiancée included. So why did he feel as if this time were the first? And why did that seem so damned important?

Because first times could never be repeated. And first *loves* never died. So now what?

Alix let out an ear-piercing shriek. Griff knew better than to ignore his niece and welcomed the few minutes alone.

"I'll get her." Without meeting her gaze, he untangled himself from Chelsie and gritted his teeth when the cool air hit his naked skin.

In silence, she slipped out of the bed and closed herself in his bathroom. He drew a steadying breath as the door clicked shut behind her. After donning a pair of jeans, he grabbed the shirt she'd been wearing. He pulled it over his head, but the chill remained.

Chelsie's warmth, which had been a part of him just minutes before, seemed long gone. And he missed her.

Griff returned quickly, before Chelsie could have a chance to formulate any regrets. The strength of what they'd shared stunned him. He knew they needed to deal with the aftereffects before either could place too much—or too little—emphasis on making love.

He plopped Alix down on the center of the mattress and rejoined Chelsie in bed. Alix rolled and flopped around on the large bed, apparently happy to be out of the confining crib.

Her dark eyes met his. From her expression, she, too, recognized that this was hardly the usual morning after. Whatever he was about to say got cut off by Alix, who threw herself into his arms. Her cheerful babble provided the only buffer between the two adults.

"Hey, squirt. What do you say you play on the floor a while. I've got some business to take care of." He placed her on the carpet beside the bed where he had a ready stack of toys for her to play with.

"No." Alix climbed back onto the bed with little agility but lots of gusto. At six-thirty in the morning, he had to admire her spunk.

Chelsie smiled, but the emotion didn't reach her eyes.

"At times like these, it's hard to imagine life with more than one kid." He ruffled Alix's soft curls with his hand.

"Is that what you want?" Chelsie asked.

He paused to think. One look at his niece and he had his answer. "Yeah." He gave Alix a playful tug on her hair.

Griff glanced at Chelsie, realizing for the first time that she had retreated to the far end of the bed. She'd changed into her sweatshirt and jeans from the day before, covering the body that he'd memorized inch by tantalizing inch. He didn't like the not-so-subtle message she projected.

"Scram, squirt," he whispered in Alix's ear. The little girl climbed between Griff and Chelsie. "Not exactly what I had in mind."

Alix smiled, showing the dimples that charmed everyone she met, then reached for Chelsie's hair. "Mommy."

Griff groaned. But to his surprise, the knife-like pain that usually accompanied Alix's pleas for her mother had dulled somewhat. In large part, he suspected, he owed that step forward to the woman sitting next to him.

"It's Aunt Chelsie. You know that." Reaching over, he ruffled the little girl's hair.

He looked over his niece's head to smile at Chelsie. She met his gaze, but in her eyes, he saw the haunted look he'd come to recognize and hate at the same time. He couldn't come up with one reason for her to have withdrawn.

"Give me a few minutes to get her settled and we'll talk," he whispered.

Chelsie shook her head. "I'm late." She scrambled out of bed.

"At"—he glanced at the clock—"six-forty? Where could you possibly have to be on a Sunday morning?"

"The shelter." She gazed at his nightstand, a ploy clearly enabling her to avoid his stare.

"I thought you were sticking around to take care of us."

She looked from Alix, who chattered happily, back

to Griff. "Both of you look much better. And clearly you have the energy to take care of her."

"So you're running away."

"Leaving for a while."

"You'll be back?"

Her silence hit him like a slap in the face. "Don't let us keep you, then."

His icy tone must have melted some of her barriers. "Please don't make this harder," she pleaded.

"Give me one good reason why I shouldn't. We went into this like two adults. As I recall, I asked you to be sure. So what's with the sudden withdrawal?"

Her frantic gaze again darted to Alix and back to him. "Just give me some space, okay? I'll be back. I promise."

"Okay." What choice did he have? He'd never force a woman who didn't want to stay and he'd never hold on to a woman in that much pain. Looking at Chelsie's trembling body, he knew that she was.

His first instinct had been to cast her in the role of villain, as the woman who deserted him like his mother and ex-fiancée. He could no longer accept that explanation. He'd come to know Chelsie well in the last few weeks, even better in the last twenty-four hours. Her role in the custody hearing no longer tortured his thoughts. She'd made her own way without the help of her parents, chosen a career that benefited others and not herself.

He even understood her role in the custody hearing now, understood why and believed her regrets. Family was important to her. The caring woman he'd come to know wouldn't turn down her parents' request for help. The irony was she'd lost them anyway. In all the time they'd been together with Alix, she'd never once

mentioned her family or their abrupt departure for
Florida. According to Ryan, charity functions were
rampant down there this time of year. Chelsie's priorities he understood. Theirs he didn't.

But there was more to Chelsie than her caring
nature. Something haunted her, had kept her from
her sister and niece before, and caused her to run
now, which led him to the possibility she was running from herself and not from him.

The probability didn't lessen the feelings of aban-
donment he'd hoped never to experience again, but
the knowledge allowed him to let her go in peace.
He, too, could use the time to sort out his jumbled
emotions.

"I'm sorry," she whispered.

He shrugged, but said nothing. Ignoring her
seemed the easiest means of blocking his pain. She
reached down and retrieved her sneakers from the
floor.

He leaned back against the pillows and shut his
eyes, waiting until he heard the thud of the bedroom door before opening them again. The noise
emphasized the point. He was alone.

EIGHT

Chelsie drove for hours, seeking solace that eluded her. She'd get lost, circle the same roads four or five times, find her way, and just keep going. She had nowhere else to turn.

Her work, always an escape, was now tied to Griff. Her office, her papers, her things all sat in boxes in the upstairs of his house. Though she could go back to the city, her tiny apartment held little appeal. She'd furnished her cold apartment as a reminder. The decor clearly stated this was no place for a child.

Until this morning, the reminder had worked. The sterile, glass environment she'd purposefully created was home to the woman she'd been before she had accepted Griffin Stuart's offer. Before she'd been foolish enough to make love with him.

That woman had known she'd never have children, a family, a warm place to call home. She'd known better than to become a part of something she could never have. The minute Griff had brought the little girl into the bed, as if they were a family, *her family,* Chelsie's orderly world had tipped precariously off balance. When he'd indicated his preference to have more children, her world disintegrated before her.

For the first time, she'd dared to want something she could never have. She should have known better. She made a U-turn and headed towards Boston. Maybe time alone in her apartment was exactly what she needed to set things right.

But when she walked into the stark, crystal-filled living room, she didn't find the sense of peace she sought. She found the truth. The place she called home wasn't. Chelsie was alone.

"I take it this is your version of 'coming back'?" Griff asked on Monday morning. The rest of the weekend had passed without a word or a phone call, as if the night they'd spent together had never happened.

"I'm here."

"It's a little late, isn't it?"

Chelsie turned from the box she'd been unpacking. "I never said when, just that I'd be here."

"Semantics again."

"Whatever."

She unwrapped a brass clock and placed it next to the blotter on her desk. He shoved his hands into his pants pockets. Otherwise, he might give in to the urge to throttle her. The woman standing before him in a prim business suit and hair pulled back into a tight bun bore little resemblance to the tousled woman in his bed the morning before. Unfortunately, her seductive scent was the same and memories flooded back hard and fast. Even her outward appearance couldn't dull his need.

He suspected she'd undergone the transformation on purpose. That she thought the cool facade would provide a deterrent only proved how little she knew him.

"How are you feeling?" she asked.

"Better."

"And Alix?"

"Also better. Mrs. Baxter's back."

"I know. I called to check on Alix earlier."

And didn't bother to speak with him. Griff reached for her arm, turning her to face him. "We have to talk."

She shook her head. "Not now." She gestured to the many boxes spread across the floor.

So she had to unpack. He knew that and had planned on helping out. His secretary had come in for a few hours and then he'd given her the rest of the day off for the same reason. There would be plenty of time for work when he and Chelsie had finished combining offices.

Without a secretary or client in sight, Griff couldn't think of a better moment to hash things out between them. "Seems like the perfect time to me. We're alone."

"But we won't be for long. While you were downstairs, your secretary left a message about booking a potential client around noon." Her lips turned downward in a frown.

"A potential client," he repeated. "And that's bad news?"

"Depends." She moved the now empty box onto the floor. "Can you hand me that one?" She pointed across the room to a brown box labeled *Personal.* "It's fragile."

He hefted the box off the floor, surprised when it lifted easily, and placed it on the desk she'd had delivered early this morning. From a basic office supply depot, the wooden desk lacked the old charm of Griff's own, and was the complete opposite of the crystal-and-glass palace Chelsie called home.

Come to think of it, he realized, glancing around at the objects she'd already unpacked, her office decor was homey and lived in, rather than sleek and untouchable. More like the Chelsie he'd come to know. The disparate looks intrigued him as much as the woman herself.

He watched as she sliced open the box with a thin razor blade. "I'd think you'd be happy I booked a new client," he said. "At least I'm pulling my weight." Or beginning to, he thought. Leaving the corporate world behind in favor of family law, he hadn't taken a single client with him from his old office. He'd wanted it that way, wanted to leave all shreds of that life and lifestyle behind.

"I would be if I thought you were prepared for this one."

"You think I can't handle a new client? If you trust me so little, why the hell did you agree to this partnership in the first place?" Why the hell had she slept with him and complicated his life even more?

"I'm not sure," she murmured. "But before you start getting defensive, you should realize something." Without meeting his gaze, she began digging through tissue paper inside the box.

More crystal? he wondered, unable to keep the disappointment from invading his mind. Had he been wrong to think the icy apartment was a sham and the warmth of her office a reflection of the real Chelsie Russell?

"This is your first domestic violence case."

Her softly spoken words halted his callous thoughts and Griff paused. Domestic violence. Her past. Abuse. Once a part of her life. What did he really know of this woman? How could he presume to judge her time and again? "So what are you suggesting?" he asked, purposefully backing off. "I'll do whatever you think is best."

She raised her gaze. "Why are you so agreeable all of a sudden?" she asked warily.

He shrugged. "Because in this area of law you know best?"

"Or because you're afraid of treading on what you now think is forbidden territory? Don't do it. If I hadn't admitted my past, what would you be telling me now?" Her eyes held a definite challenge.

The spark had returned and Griff liked it. "I'd say I could handle it," he admitted.

"And I'm telling you, you can't. Not without guidance the first time."

"Why?" he asked, pushing her just as she'd requested.

She didn't want to be pampered. He respected that. If she wanted to force him into being his obstinate, lawyerly self, he'd comply. If they were going to be partners, neither one could afford to let the other call the shots without good reason. "Considering I've been dealing with clients since before graduating law school, and knowing that most of them are stubborn and egotistical, why would you presume to think I couldn't handle this one?"

"For exactly those reasons." She squared her shoulders, a defensive stance probably meant to prove she could hold her own with him. "All your experience means zero around here. You may be a corporate wiz and you could probably challenge the toughest CEO and win, but that mentality won't work in family law. You know nothing about the psyche of these women. You don't know what makes them run away from the abuse or back to it. The slightest error in word choice could compromise not only your securing a new client, but her life as well." She met and held his gaze for a brief moment before digging through the box once more.

Griff remained silent. The crinkle of tissue paper was the only sound in the now quiet room. Easing himself onto the far edge of her desk, he thought about her words. A smile pulled at his lips. She was good. Damned good. Too bad he was trained to recognize her game. She'd stroked his ego in his area of expertise while asserting authority in her own.

As frustrated as he was with her personally right now, he knew without a doubt he was going to enjoy working with Chelsie Russell. He was also going to learn about humility, because to his amazement, and despite his slightly bruised ego, he admitted to himself she was right. He couldn't handle this first case. Not alone.

He needed Chelsie.

He cleared his throat, intending to tell her, at the same time she finally unwrapped the contents of the box.

Sentiment had no place in her life, Chelsie thought. So why had she decided to bring this collection here? And why now?

Although she felt Griff's steady gaze, he remained silent. For that she was grateful. One at a time, she unwrapped the tiny silver frames holding the cherished pictures of herself and her sister. In keeping with her sister's love of keeping personal accounts, every year Chelsie had given Shannon a leather-bound diary for Christmas. Every year, Shannon had given Chelsie a framed picture of them as children, along with a humorous label at the bottom. The tradition continued even after Chelsie's marriage and divorce. The only difference was the UPS man was the carrier instead of Chelsie. When she'd grabbed this box from the floor of her closet early this morning, Chelsie told herself it was for Alix.

She'd lied.

Griff was chipping away at the protective layers she'd built around herself. He was making her feel. She didn't know whether to love him or hate him for that, since it also meant she'd be facing another loss when *they* ended.

She placed the mini-frames on her desk. Griff's hand covered hers. Warmth and comfort flooded her. Too soon he moved to take the picture from her hand. He studied the photo, the only one that included her parents, taken when Chelsie and Shannon had been almost too young to remember.

"You look like a regular happy family."

She shrugged. "Maybe we were. Maybe something got warped along the way. I know they loved us. Their priorities shifted at some point. They do love Alix."

"I believe you."

Because he spoke without hesitation, she believed him, too.

He lowered the frame to her desk. "You miss them."

"They're my parents."

"It's more than that, and we both know it." He'd

come up behind her. Solid and steady, he aroused both her deep feelings of need and a purely sexual humming she couldn't seem to ignore. Problem was, it had gotten her into deep waters yesterday. She looked at the tiny silver mementos once more. He'd drawn her in so deep she'd pulled out her past and brought it around to face her present.

Although she might be ready for that, she wasn't ready to face Griff and explain why she'd left him so abruptly.

He circled her and settled himself back on the edge of her desk, putting distance between them. Had he sensed her unease?

"I think you're right about this next appointment," he said.

Chelsie figured he'd pegged her discomfort for what it was. Although he'd granted her a reprieve, she knew it was temporary. "How so?" she asked.

"I'd like to think I can handle this, but I'm not going to risk my client's safety or security on ego. I'd like you to be there."

She nodded, impressed with his ability to put someone else first. Impressed with him. "I'll sit in."

He shook his head. "Not just sit in. I'll take my cues from you."

She knew it was a big concession. "I'm glad you realize your client's needs come first. You'll be handling these cases alone in no time."

"When, Chelsie?"

"There's no time frame for these kinds of things. See how you feel after today and . . ."

He cut her off with an abrupt wave of her hand. "I meant when can we talk about us?"

His definition of temporary and hers differed

greatly. She gripped the edge of her desk, unable and unwilling to delve into her heart and soul just yet. "Later."

His eyes narrowed at her words. "Pick a time."

A knock sounded at the door. She took a step forward, but he was faster, stepping into her path. His large body blocked her chance of moving forward and his waist came into sudden contact with hers. She let out a startled gasp. The knock came, louder this time.

"Just a second," Griff called. He fingered the pink bow on her silk shirt. His hand grazed her cheek. "Pick a time."

"Lunch," she said through clenched teeth.

"Perfect." He took two steps backwards, watching as she smoothed her bow with what she knew were shaking hands. "Do you want to get that or should I?" he asked.

"I've got it." She needed the few seconds to compose herself. Chelsie brushed past him and opened the door.

A woman around Chelsie's age stood before them. "Hi. I'm early, but I had to take the bus and I wasn't sure how long it would take."

"Come in," Chelsie said. "Welcome to Russell and Stuart."

"Stuart and Russell," Griff said from behind, but she heard the laughter in his voice.

"We haven't worked out all the details yet, but come on in." Chelsie waved the woman inside.

She entered, her eyes never leaving Chelsie's face. Reassurance was important. Chelsie understood that firsthand.

"We can talk in my office," Griff said, taking charge.

"Unless you'd be more comfortable out here," Chelsie said, giving the woman choices she'd probably been lacking lately.

Their client looked from Chelsie to Griff and back again. "His office is fine, if you come."

Chelsie nodded and the woman stepped back to allow Griff to lead her through the waiting area into his office. Despite the wariness in the woman's eyes, Chelsie noticed a regal bearing, a notch of pride that hadn't yet been taken from her.

Watching them precede her, Chelsie saw their surroundings as if for the first time. A worn couch, plush but unobtrusive beige carpet, a small reception area, a coffee machine and water cooler. Except for the massive oak desk he'd taken before leaving his old partnership behind, Griff's private office looked much the same.

She suppressed a smile. Until now, she hadn't realized how Griff had decorated to suit his new clientele. No luxuries to make those without feel out of place, but chic enough to allow people with money to believe they'd sought out an equal in their attorney. Much like the downstairs unit he and Alix called home, this place spoke of class that had nothing to do with status and everything to do with its owner.

Chelsie waited for the woman to seat herself before settling in the chair next to hers. Instead of retreating behind his imposing desk, Griff chose a spot on the couch. The woman seemed to relax a bit. Again, Chelsie had to commend his instincts.

"Would you like to take off your coat?" Chelsie asked.

The woman shrugged off an expensive-looking burgundy silk jacket, proof that spousal abuse crossed economic and social boundaries. How well she knew that. "Mrs. . . ." Chelsie paused. She had forgotten to check Griff's appointment book for the woman's name, if she had even given it.

"Amanda."

"Okay." From experience, Chelsie knew that being on a first-name basis gave her clients the impression of anonymity while they decided whether they trusted her enough to tell all. "You called us, Amanda, so what can we do for you?"

"I know I set this appointment up with Mr. Stuart . . ."

"I can leave you alone if you're comfortable now," Chelsie offered in a soft voice. Inspiring trust was the only way to insure a client's confidence.

"No!"

"Okay. Why don't you start at the beginning?"

The woman gripped the edges of her chair until her knuckles turned white. "I have a little boy," she whispered. "If it weren't for him, I don't know if I'd be here."

Chelsie nodded. "I know this first step was difficult. How old is your son?" Chelsie asked.

"Three. And I don't want . . ."

Silence surrounded them, but Chelsie waited. She hoped Griff would take his cue from her and do the same. He leaned forward in his seat, but remained quiet.

Slowly, the woman unbuttoned one sleeve of her cotton blouse, lifting the cuff to reveal angry bruises on her arm. "I've lived with this for so long, but I couldn't bear it if he hurt my little boy."

Though she felt the heat of his gaze, Chelsie refused to look at Griff. He knew when they'd become partners he'd be taking on cases like these, and she'd promised her expertise from the beginning. But that had been before she'd revealed her own personal history. His request had been based on her experience with battered women. Now that he knew she fell into the category of the abused, Chelsie couldn't cope with his pity.

She forced herself to focus on Amanda, to look at the bruises, so similar to the ones Chelsie's own husband had left on her upper arms.

"It takes courage for you to be here, Amanda. Where's your son now?" Griff asked.

"With a friend."

"Okay. What do you want from us?" Chelsie asked. The words, the decision had to come from the woman herself. No one could force her to press charges or file for divorce or any of her other options unless *she* wanted to. Chelsie had learned that from personal experience as well.

"I left three days ago, when I first called you. I'm staying with a friend, but I can't put her in such a compromising position much longer. Every time the phone rings, I jump. Each time someone hangs up or breathes heavily, I think it's him."

"You have options," Chelsie assured her. "The first is to continue to stay with friends or relatives, but I tend to agree with you, and I don't recommend that for now."

The other woman nodded.

"The second is a much more difficult decision,

but wiser in the long run. There's a women's shelter. I volunteer there, so I know it well. You'd be safe and your friends wouldn't be in any danger. Once we decide how to proceed, depending upon the course of action we take, you could always return home or to a friend or family member."

Amanda's face went pale at the mention of the shelter. Chelsie had been right. The concept drove reality home. Sometimes, facing the truth, realizing you had to rebuild a life alone, was more difficult than an actual physical beating.

"Do you have any money?" Chelsie asked. Despite the woman's expensive clothing, whether she'd managed to leave with any personal belongings or cash was anybody's guess.

"Not much. I still have my credit cards, though."

"No. No paper trails." Chelsie took the woman's hand. "Do you trust me?" she asked.

"Implicitly." Amanda spoke without hesitation.

"Good. Then we have to do things my way. Not only for your safety and your son's, but also for the courts. Agreed?"

Amanda nodded. Griff rose and seated himself behind his desk, pulling out a legal pad and pen.

"We'll need some information," he said, refocusing on work.

After drawing a deep breath, Amanda nodded. "Okay."

"I need your full name."

The other woman looked towards Chelsie, who nodded in encouragement. "Amanda Davis . . ." She hesitated before continuing. "Amanda Davis Sutton."

Chelsie's vision blurred and she sucked in a deep

breath. Coincidence, she told herself. A brief glance told her Griff was jotting down pertinent information.

"Your husband's name?" Griff asked.

"Jeffrey Sutton."

Chelsie glanced at Amanda, hoping she was wrong. The other woman met her gaze and nodded almost imperceptibly.

Jeff Sutton. Nausea roiled in Chelsie's stomach. The one slice of dried toast she'd managed to choke down for breakfast threatened to come back up. She swallowed over the lump in her throat and asked, "How long have you been married?"

"Four and a half years."

Griff continued to take notes. He hadn't yet appeared to notice anything amiss.

"Your husband's occupation?" Chelsie asked. She forced the question from somewhere deep inside her.

Amanda choked on a laugh. "Attorney."

"For what firm?" But she already knew. This was no coincidence. And judging by the woman's penetrating stare, Amanda knew that, as well.

"Stevens and McLaughlin, downtown Boston."

Chelsie stood. Her gaze darted from the bruises on Amanda's arm to the rest of her well-dressed but well-covered body. The nausea threatened again. "Excuse me," she murmured. "I'll be right back."

Her fault. And this time, a flesh-and-blood child's welfare was at stake. *Her fault.* The litany in her brain refused to subside.

Chelsie ran, barely making it to the bathroom in time. Afterwards, she washed her face and drank a glass of water, but she couldn't stop shaking or control the erratic beat of her heart. The cold sweat that had begun earlier now left her chilled.

With no choice, she dried her eyes and walked back into Griff's office, ignoring his concerned expression.

"I'm sorry." She glanced at Griff. "Have you gotten the rest of the information?"

He nodded.

"Good. Amanda," Chelsie said gently, "have you given any thought to what comes next?"

"I'd like to look at the shelter, if you don't mind."

"Not at all. I'm free from now through lunch, if that's okay."

"Fine."

Griff cleared his throat, but Chelsie refused to acknowledge their change in plans.

"Okay. Aside from where you'll be staying, what are you willing to do?" Chelsie asked.

"Anything necessary to protect myself and my child."

"A restraining order would be a start. Documentation of the history of abuse and pictures of any current bruises would also help. Friends' affidavits, things that would support your case in court—if you're willing to press charges."

The other woman dropped her head in her hands, but when she looked up, Chelsie saw a determination she herself hadn't had when faced with similar questions. Maybe if she'd come to her senses sooner, if she'd left Jeffrey after the first time or immediately after realizing she was pregnant, she never would have lost her baby.

Or her future, she thought, glancing at Griff.

"Whatever is necessary," Amanda reiterated.

"Good." Grasping her purse, Chelsie gestured towards the door. Amanda stood.

Griff rose from his seat, but Chelsie refused to even glance in his direction. She couldn't deal with his questioning looks. Not now. He walked over and placed his arm around Amanda's shoulders, leading her into the waiting room. "I'd like to speak with my partner. Will you be all right?" he asked.

"Fine."

He nodded. "Help yourself to coffee."

"Thank you."

"You're welcome. We'll be right with you."

Griff turned to Chelsie. Before she could make an excuse to avoid any discussion, his hand firmly grasped her wrist. "Inside," he whispered.

Anxiety caused her to plant her feet firmly in the doorway.

"Now, please."

Faced with the choice of upsetting Amanda with a scene or dealing with Griff, Chelsie turned and walked back into his office.

NINE

"I can't help if you won't talk to me."

Chelsie stood with her back to Griff and stared out the window. A slight breeze blew the branches on the trees and she wished she were outside enjoying the end of summer, instead of being inside, subjected to an early frost.

"What happened back there?" he demanded in a no-nonsense tone.

She shrugged. "Something I ate didn't agree with me. I'm okay now."

He cleared his throat and she heard him restlessly pacing the carpet behind her. Though her half-answers might frustrate him, she had no choice but to stall. With a client waiting outside, she couldn't get into personal matters, but with personal intruding on business, she realized she couldn't put off the inevitable much longer.

"Are you sure it didn't have something more to do with the subject matter?" he asked, his voice softening.

"Two days ago, you wouldn't have asked me that question."

"Two days ago, you hadn't confided in me. Two days ago, we hadn't made love."

Her body heated with the memory and his genuine concern tugged at her heart. She could no longer avoid him, but she couldn't bear a pitying look in his eyes, either. She whirled around, finally facing him, only to discover deep emotion lingered in the hazel depths. Pity was nowhere to be found.

"Tell me something, Griff. Does having sex give you the right to grill me?"

She regretted the words the minute they left her mouth. The entire situation had her rattled, which was no excuse to take her rampaging emotions out on the man she loved.

To his credit, he merely shrugged out of his suit jacket and tossed it over a chair. She recognized the delay as a means to bide time and calm his anger. She gave him his due. How a man could be just as devastating fully dressed as he had been unclothed baffled her. But it was the man inside the clothes that had drawn her out and made her fall in love.

When he met her stare, his expression darkened, along with his eyes. He took two steps forward, but she stopped him mid-stride with as much honesty as she could muster.

"I'm sorry, please forget I said that." She lifted her hand and worked the sore muscles in the back of her neck. "Yes, the subject matter is upsetting," she said, lowering herself into the nearest chair. She owed Griff as much of the truth as she felt he could handle hearing—as much as she could handle revealing—for now.

His hand touched her cheek. "I don't like seeing you hurt. Do you react like this after every client interview?"

She shook her head, unwittingly freeing some

strands of hair. Without much thought, she tucked them behind her ear. "Some hit me harder than others."

"No wonder this one's difficult. She looks so much like you. The dark hair, the eyes . . ."

"I hadn't noticed." And she hadn't. Now that he'd pointed out their similarities, Chelsie realized Griff was right—another factor that must have unconsciously upset her. "I really must have eaten something that didn't agree with me, or else I'm catching a new version of the virus you and Alix had." Which wasn't a lie, since her throat had been raw all morning. "I'll be all right."

"Want me to accompany you to the shelter?" he asked.

Her lips curved upward in a faint smile. "No, thanks. No men allowed, anyway."

Griff knelt down beside her. He enclosed her hand in his. "We do have unfinished business."

"I know." She shut her eyes and leaned her head back in the chair. "But would you understand if I said I'm not up to discussing things yet?"

He answered with a tender but brief kiss. His lips, warm against hers, almost seduced her into a blessed state of forgetfulness. Before she was ready, he pulled back, leaving her bereft.

"In case you weren't sure, that's a yes," he said.

"I'm shocked, but thank you."

"Don't be. As long as you don't run out on me again, I can give you all the space you need. To be honest, I could use some myself." He rose from his kneeling position, putting both physical and emotional distance between them.

He'd admitted to nothing more than she asked for herself, yet his admission and withdrawal hurt.

"I've got to get back to Amanda," she said.

"I have a favor to ask first."

"What is it?"

"Ryan asked me to help his sister move back in with her husband next weekend. As you know, I owe him. Mrs. Baxter promised Saturday to her son and daughter-in-law. Think you could . . ."

"Baby-sit?" she asked with a grin. "Sure. Would you mind if I took Alix into Boston with me?"

"Either you're brave or just plain nuts, but no, I don't mind. Thanks."

"Friends help each other out, Griff." She needed to cement their status in her own mind, as much as his.

"Is that all we are?"

"I thought this discussion could wait," she chided. The real world would not. The life she thought she'd put behind her waited outside the safety of these walls.

"Not for long."

Ignoring his words, Chelsie slipped out the office door.

"How did you find me?" Chelsie asked the woman in the passenger seat of her car. Chelsie wanted enough details to understand what she would be dealing with.

"I searched through Jeffrey's drawers and files for spare money or something that could help me. I came across your divorce decree."

"He hadn't told you he'd been married?"

"No."

Chelsie spared a quick glance at Amanda, then refocused on the road. The woman's dark hair fell to her shoulders. Griff was right. From a distance, they could have passed for sisters.

"But now that I've met you, I can see why he married me," Amanda said.

"Whoa. There was no love lost by the time we divorced. I can assure you, Jeff would not marry someone who reminded him of me."

"But he would marry someone he had no trouble manipulating, who did as he said without question."

Chelsie slowed the car in the back parking lot of the women's shelter. After shutting off the engine, she turned toward the woman beside her. "You may have done those things, but you got out. You saved yourself and your son. Be proud instead of kicking yourself for things you can't change." She smiled. "Counselors here will help you see that you aren't the one with the problem. He is."

"You'll help me, too?"

"I'll do everything I can within the law, but I think it's better if Griff handles the specifics. Ethically, you don't want anything Jeff can hold over you. Having his ex-wife represent you might pose a problem. Anyway, you did set the appointment up with Griff."

"Only because I thought you might figure out who I was and refuse to see me. I wanted to tell you in person."

"Did you tell Griff?"

"No. I wanted to talk to you first."

"Would you mind if I handled that in my own way?" Chelsie asked.

Amanda shook her head.

Somehow, Chelsie would have to explain. Because

she'd withdrawn her complaint against her husband for purely selfish reasons, she had freed him to abuse someone else. It wasn't something she could admit lightly, but she did need to see the past rectified. Now she had her chance.

In the process, maybe she'd even ease some of the guilt that had been building inside her for years. Until faced with Amanda's courage to walk out before any harm came to her child, Chelsie hadn't realized what a huge burden she'd been carrying.

Time to face her past, she thought, as well as herself. To do that, she had to begin with being honest.

Chelsie turned towards Amanda. "If you need anything, someone to talk to or whatever, don't hesitate to call." After rummaging through her purse, Chelsie withdrew an old business card. Though Amanda probably already had the number, Chelsie jotted down Griff's office phone just in case. "You can reach me here, or leave a message. I check in periodically." Chelsie paused. "Call anytime."

Fingering the card in her hand, Amanda gave Chelsie a grateful smile. "Thanks."

"You're welcome. One more question before we go in."

"What?"

"Why me? Why look me up? Why ask me to represent you?"

The other woman stared out the window. "The night before I left, I confronted Jeff with the fact that he'd been married. We argued about his lie, and I asked him why you divorced." She paused, obviously uncomfortable with the rest.

Chelsie could handle whatever came next. As far

as she was concerned, the worst had already befallen her.

"He said his—I mean, he said your work came first."

A grim smile touched Chelsie's lips. "Please don't sugarcoat this for my sake." She'd heard Jeffrey at his most vulgar, maybe not in the beginning of their marriage, but certainly at the bitter end. "Be honest, please."

Amanda sucked in a breath of air. "He said his frigid wife saved her passion for her work. She couldn't manage to satisfy him in bed." Slowly, Amanda turned away from the window. "If Jeffrey bothered to belittle your career, I figured you must be good." Regret for her admission etched her delicate features. "I'm sorry," she whispered.

Chelsie shrugged. There might have been a time she believed those words. Jeff had told her the same thing many times in the course of their short marriage. But one night with Griff taught her how very wrong her ex-husband had been.

Chelsie now knew she hadn't saved her passion for her work. She had saved it for someone deserving. Someone named Griff.

Early Saturday morning, Griff buzzed her apartment from downstairs. Chelsie'd had barely enough time to shower and change after her night at the woman's shelter downtown before he'd arrived. She let him and Alix, who swung monkey-style from his left arm, into her apartment.

"You know, you're becoming a master at avoidance techniques."

"Good morning to you, too," she said, but she

nodded. "I can see how you'd think that, but take a look at my schedule for the last week and tell me where we could have fit in time for a long, personal, *important* conversation."

"We couldn't, which brings me back to my original point. Did you arrange the week on purpose?"

"To avoid you? No. To make sure Amanda got settled at the shelter? Yes." She had spent three of the last four nights there, helping the other woman out and even getting to know her little boy. In between, she'd fit in quick dinners with Alix, not to mention her already scheduled appointments. She'd seen Griff constantly, but not once had they been alone.

"I respect your work. I just think we have unfinished business."

Again, she nodded. She couldn't avoid him much longer. In truth, she didn't want to. She respected him too much to continue as they'd been. "We just need to find some quiet time—"

As if on cue, Alix squealed loudly, released Griff, and scrambled into Chelsie's arms. The little girl wouldn't be ignored. Chelsie laughed. "See?"

With an exasperated groan, Griff gave in and grinned before glancing at his watch. "I've got to go. Are you sure you can handle this? I can call Ryan. He'd understand."

"I think I've had enough practice."

"What if she needs a nap? She's still in a crib."

"I'll put her in my bed, surround her with pillows, and I won't leave her alone." She held up her hands. "Promise."

Restless and bored with the adult conversation, Alix bolted for the living room. Chelsie let her go.

"What about all that crystal?" His gaze swept the

expanse of her apartment. His reluctance to leave Alix in this crystal palace was a tangible thing. The little girl rushed from place to place, lifting each animal and replacing it with a heavy thud.

"Alix!" he shouted.

Chelsie jabbed her elbow into his side. "Leave her alone. She isn't doing anything wrong. Maybe I should have taken the things down, for safety's sake, but as long as I'm here, she's fine. Just go."

"Are you sure you're feeling better?"

Though she tried, Chelsie couldn't suppress a smirk. "I had a slight cold and worked straight through. You, on the other hand, took to bed. Obviously, I have more stamina."

He groaned at the words she'd been teasing him with all week.

She sent him a reassuring smile. "Good-bye," she said in a lilting voice. Placing her hands on his back, she shoved him towards the door. A denim jacket separated her fingers from his skin, but heat radiated through her anyway. Just being near Griff was akin to lighting a quick-burning fire.

"I'll be back around four."

"We'll be here."

"In one piece?"

Chelsie rolled her eyes. He took the hint and left, closing the door behind him.

Chelsie glanced at Alix. "How about your first all-girl shopping trip?" she asked her niece. "I know this great place in Faneuil Hall. All teddy bears, soft and cuddly like you." Chelsie tickled the child's tummy until she shrieked in delight.

The ringing of the telephone cut off any further play and Chelsie grabbed for the receiver. "Hello?"

Silence greeted her. She wondered if Griff had called to check from his car phone already. "Hello?" she said again. "Griff?" No answer. "Bad connection," she muttered. She had a hard time dialing out from her mobile phone around here too.

"Serves Uncle Griff right for not trusting us," Chelsie said. She looked at Alix. "But we love him anyway, right?"

When Griff reached Chelsie's apartment, he found the door ajar. "That woman needs a keeper," he muttered to himself. A role he wouldn't mind applying for himself. All afternoon, his mind had been on the two females he'd left behind. Though he trusted Chelsie with Alix, he didn't trust his niece in Chelsie's apartment. More than once, his own mother had nearly throttled Griff or Jared if they'd even looked at one of her *souvenirs*.

The one time Jared had done real damage to a precious trinket, Griff had taken the blame for his kid brother. A mere three days later, his mother had walked out for good. Since then, Griff's taste and eye had been honed by years of making money and dealing with women who respected little else. The items in Chelsie's place appeared more valuable than those coveted by his mother.

As he stepped into the tiled entryway, hushed voices and soft giggles drifted towards him. Not wishing to interrupt, Griff entered the apartment quietly and came upon a sight that not only astounded him, but altered his perception of reality.

The glass cocktail tables that previously occupied the center of the living room had been haphazardly pushed aside. Every glass and crystal animal, numbering twenty or more, sat on the carpet surrounding his niece. Alix held two in her hands and proceeded to bang them together like cymbals. He winced each time they struck. The lead inside the crystal must have prevented them from shattering.

"Don't, sweety. You'll get hurt." Chelsie gently pried the animals from the little girl's grasp. Where he was worried about Chelsie's things, she was worried about the little girl's safety. The discrepancy should have surprised him, but didn't.

"Okay. Teddy bear," Chelsie said.

Alix lifted an animal off the floor.

"Fish. Try again."

As he took a step towards them, something crunched under his feet. The noise drew their attention from the menagerie on the floor.

"Griff!" Chelsie jumped up to greet him. The joy in her voice was unmistakable and he was glad he'd entered in silence. She'd had no time to think, so her spontaneous gesture had been genuine. A warm yet alien feeling flooded his heart. For the first time, Griff felt like he'd come home.

Alix darted around Chelsie's legs and ran into his arms. The child's unconditional love never ceased to amaze him and enabled him to give in return.

"Hi, ladies. How was your day?"

"Eventful."

He nodded. Alix pried herself from his grasp and headed straight for the animals. He stepped forward and again, his foot ground something against the floor. "What's this?" he asked, looking down.

"Nothing important. I just haven't had a chance to clean up yet." Chelsie gnawed on her lower lip before rushing on. "But don't worry. I was with Alix the whole time and she never got near the broken glass. I'll get it now."

He stopped her run for the closet by grabbing the tail of her shirt. "Relax. It was a simple question, not an accusation. I know you'd never let Alix get hurt. But did she break this?"

"An accident." Laughter twinkled in Chelsie's eyes. "The animals wanted to play follow the leader. I'm afraid the rabbit was a bit uncooperative."

The rabbit. Her favorite piece, yet she seemed not to care. "I'll replace it."

"No, you won't. I don't care about these things. Alix had fun. That's all that matters."

His eyes narrowed as he assessed her sincerity.

"Honest, Griff. Don't make a big deal about this. I never thought a small accident would affect you like this."

You affect me. Who was this woman who never reacted in accordance with the standards set by the women in his past? "Okay. We'll forget it for now."

A brief flash of relief crossed her face. "Good. You hungry? We could order in pizza before you go home."

He glanced across the room. Alix still played contentedly in the center of the carpet. "Pizza sounds good."

Chelsie picked up the phone and placed the order.

"Want to sit?" She flopped down on the couch and waited until he joined her. He groaned, his exhaustion evident in the slouch of his shoulders and the weary expression on his face.

Alix ran to Griff, dumping two animals in his lap. She continued to charge back and forth between her uncle and the pile of crystals she thought of as toys. When Chelsie glanced at the heap in the center of the floor, she decided this activity might take a while. It might take even longer for the memory of Griff and Alix in her apartment to fade, she thought with chagrin.

"What's our game plan for Amanda Sutton's case, partner?" he asked.

"Let's discuss business later." She nodded towards Alix. She couldn't talk about the details of their newest client without revealing all the details of her past, something she wouldn't do without a guarantee of privacy. Now wasn't the time. The coward in her heart, a shadow of her former self, welcomed the delay.

"Okay, the squirt comes first," he said, settling himself on the carpet beside Alix.

Chelsie's heart swelled at the sight of the two people she had come to love frolicking on her living-room floor. Griff and Alix in her apartment created the illusion of a real home, something this place would never be.

Griff glanced up, his gaze locking with hers. "Come join us. We need you."

His words sent a tingle along her spine. She liked that he'd linked them together in something other than a professional capacity. In fact, she enjoyed the notion too much. Maybe the sound pleased her because he'd said "us" without conscious thought.

She sat between them. After a while, Alix laid her head in Chelsie's lap. "I love this squirt," Chelsie whispered. She fingered the dark curls, watching as the little girl's eyes grew heavy and finally closed.

"Peaceful," Griff said.

Chelsie smiled. With Alix around, a moment of

silence was rare. "This is nice," she agreed. Too nice. Maybe it was just as well the end had come. At this point, occasional visits might benefit everyone. Alix shouldn't come to rely on her any more than she already did, especially since she'd probably be making herself scarce once Griff understood everything about Chelsie Russell.

As if he read her somber mood, he spoke. "Hey." He tipped her chin upward so her eyes met his. "You are the world's best baby-sitter. And how many women get this kind of practice before they're officially called Mommy?" His lips touched hers before he turned his attention back to the sleeping child.

"Thank you," she murmured.

He turned toward her. "For what?"

For reminding me of my place. "For being so understanding," she said.

He smiled. "I'm an understanding guy."

Hold that thought. Chelsie wished she felt nearly as confident that his words would hold true.

Griff lifted the sleeping child out of her car seat and stifled a yawn. Chelsie followed him into the house. While he got Alix settled in bed, Chelsie waited downstairs. He found her in the den. Her feet were propped on an ottoman and she lounged comfortably on the couch.

"You didn't need to come all the way back with us, but I appreciate the company." He stretched his arms above his head, feeling every muscle that had worked loading boxes that afternoon. "Mrs. Baxter will be back in the morning and I'm hoping this household will resettle itself into a routine."

Her eyes followed his every movement, stirring his

body to life. Wanting Chelsie had become as much a part of him as breathing. Fantasy had been easier. Now he knew the feel of her silken skin gliding beneath him.

She smiled. "Routines are easy to fall into." She paused. "Now that Alix is asleep, we need to talk."

"Personally, I can think of other things to do while Alix sleeps." Too much time had passed and he couldn't forget the feel of Chelsie in his arms, couldn't stop the need to have her again.

Her eyes glazed over at his words and he knew she was remembering. The memories of that one night seared his mind, heated his body, and made treating her in a casual, nonlover-like manner damned difficult. Daydreams as potent as his seemed awfully real sometimes, especially those involving Chelsie Russell.

He stepped closer and placed an arm on either side of her shoulders. Her tongue darted over her lips, moistening them until they glistened.

"Talk, Griff. This shouldn't wait."

He kissed her mid-sentence, capturing her mouth with his and slipping his tongue through her already parted lips. She raised her hands to his chest in a half-hearted effort to push him away. Her hands lingered, but didn't move. Her scent surrounded him.

He needed more. He nipped lightly at her lower lip. Her hands grasped his shirt and pulled him closer, until he ended up lying on top of her on the couch.

Raising his head, he intended to stop only long enough to straighten their awkward position.

"Griff." Her throaty voice startled him.

"Give us one more night," he said. "We'll talk in the morning, I promise. Whatever it is can wait."

Uncertainty flickered in the depths of her dark eyes. He brushed a kiss over each lid, wanting her to feel gentle persuasion, not pressure. "One more night."

"We never spoke about the last night," she murmured on a soft sigh. Her body turned to liquid beneath his. Victory, which had been so uncertain minutes before, was now within his grasp.

"You talk too much, counselor," he said with a groan. But he recognized the irony in her statement. After their last encounter, he had wanted to talk about why she had fled. At this moment, any discussion on his end would be nothing more than an incoherent jumble. Despite the unsettled state of their relationship, he wanted her again, and he had to trust that she wouldn't run.

"Tomorrow, we'll leave Alix with Mrs. Baxter and you can talk as much as you want." He nibbled on her earlobe. "If you still have the energy."

She tipped her head backwards, baring her slender neck to his hungry gaze. "And I take it you intend to see that I don't?"

"Let's just say I won't be sorry if that's the end result." With the tip of his tongue, he traced a long line from the base of her neck to the sensitive spot behind her ear. She trembled beneath him. He shifted positions until his erection pressed into the juncture of her thighs.

She sucked in a deep breath. "Okay." Her capitulation came out sounding more like a husky groan. "But no matter what, we will talk tomorrow. I'll find the energy."

He laughed aloud. "We'll see about that."

Chelsie knew that she would make sure they spoke no matter what. Tomorrow. For tonight, she wanted

Griff, wanted this last time to call theirs. The whole day had been perfect. If she could look back on these last twenty-four hours as the time she'd had a family, she might survive what was to come. When he discovered the sordid details of her life, it would change the way he looked at her forever. Besides, he deserved decent memories, too. She wanted him to know she cared, even if she couldn't express her love in words.

She gazed into his dark eyes. "I won't run this time," she promised.

Gratitude for her honesty flickered across his face. Chelsie couldn't offer him much, but he deserved more than she'd given so far. She couldn't expect Griff to understand something she'd kept so carefully hidden from him. But tomorrow, he'd know everything.

"Thank you."

"I shouldn't have left last time."

"Tomorrow," he reminded her. "We'll deal with it tomorrow." Without awaiting a response, he laced his fingers through her hair, cradling her head in his hands and capturing her mouth in a kiss that robbed her of the ability to think, yet heightened her capacity to feel.

The last time had been a slow learning process for them both. This time, their movements were rushed and frantic. The last time had been marked by intimate preliminaries. This time, by unspoken mutual consent, they shed their clothing, desiring nothing more than to be joined as one.

Griff thrust into her, burying himself as deep as her body would allow. Yet despite the physical need that drove them, Chelsie felt an intense rush of sensation flood her heart and her mind. Almost, she thought, as if the most intimate part of her body had a direct channel to her heart. And Griff had penetrated both.

Griff awoke with a start. Chelsie slept curled beside him, her head on his chest. With every breath he took, he inhaled the sweet scent of her shampoo. In sleep, she looked more trusting. Yet he felt a barrier had tumbled in the last few hours. In a very real sense, she had given herself to him, heart and soul. The question was, what did he intend to do with the gift?

The day he had won the custody hearing, the path of his life had been bleak but certain. His future held nothing except the promise of raising Alix. He had planned to focus on that one ray of sunshine and block out the need for anything more. So what had changed?

Not his past. His brother was gone, taken by an unfair twist of fate. Jared would never willingly have left his only child. Not so for Griff's mother. She, too, was long gone. As Ryan had discovered on Jared's request, she had died an unhappy and lonely woman. Ultimately, she had given up her family in search of an elusive dream that had never materialized. His father had passed away a few years back.

Instead of learning from the past, Griff had merely repeated it. Like his mother, his ex-fiancée was a woman short on feelings for anything except cold hard cash. Why had he ever thought Deidre would be different? He hadn't, he realized with a sudden flash of insight. Griff had chosen her because she exhibited the same traits as his mother. Because when she left him, too, he could say he'd expected it all along.

Chelsie stirred and he pulled the blanket up around her shoulders. Her naked body snuggled closer into his embrace. Being right offered little comfort in the middle of the night. But for now, with Chelsie beside him, Griff was no longer alone—physically or emotionally.

No woman had ever made him face his past, had ever reached inside him. Chelsie touched the man who wanted love but feared being abandoned. He understood that now. Was he ready to put aside his preconceived notions and past hurts and try again?

Damned if he knew. The living-room clock chimed five. At that moment, the only thing he felt sure of was that he didn't want Mrs. Baxter to arrive and find them naked in the den.

He untangled himself from her body and stood. When he lifted her into his arms, her eyelids fluttered open. "Go back to sleep," he whispered, walking towards his bedroom.

She mumbled something unintelligible, then twined her arms around his neck and buried her head on his shoulder. Trust wasn't something she gave easily, either. For the moment, however, she did seem to trust him.

Would her faith last into the waking hours of the morning? He had no answers. When they had their talk, he hoped they'd each do their best not to undermine the progress they'd made—and not to hurt each other in the process.

TEN

Griff placed a hand on the sheets, only to discover they felt cool to his touch. He didn't panic. Chelsie had promised him she wouldn't run and he believed her.

He started down the long hallway. When he'd bought the house, he'd tried to imbue the place with warmth and felt he had succeeded everywhere except for the kitchen. Even with Alix's high chair and bibs strewn about, the room still felt cold. With a table large enough to seat eight and no feminine knickknacks lying about, the place looked as welcoming as his old bachelor-style apartment.

When he reached the kitchen, he immediately sensed a difference. An old Eagles song drifted towards him, accompanied by soft but slightly off-key humming. Griff paused in the doorway, attempting to understand the comforting feeling that settled around him.

The decor hadn't changed. In fact, the scene that awaited him was similar to the one that greeted him every morning. Alix sat in the high chair, happily shoveling handfuls of food into her mouth while babbling at the same time. Two places were set at the table, and the delicious aroma of pancakes surrounded him, making his mouth water for a hot stack with warm maple syrup and steaming coffee. But instead of Mrs. Baxter helping his niece with her meal and puttering around the kitchen, there was Chelsie.

Between sips of coffee, she wrestled with Alix as the child tried to stuff in more food than her mouth would hold. Chelsie laughed at the little girl, gently chiding her for misbehaving. Yet Chelsie never lost her temper and she never seemed annoyed at being placed in the role of caregiver for her sister's child. If anything, she seemed born to be Alix's surrogate mother.

The emotions roiling inside Griff were too complex to untangle, so he didn't try. Instead, he studied her in silence.

She'd pulled her hair loosely atop her head and stray tendrils fell to frame her face. He had to stifle the urge to sweep her off her feet and back into the bedroom so they could pick up where they'd left off last night.

"Morning," he said, finally.

Chelsie jumped in her seat. "Morning." She turned towards him.

Despite last night's intimacy, or perhaps because of it, a pink flush covered her cheeks. He found her shyness around him a refreshing change from the overly confident women in his past.

"You should have wakened me."

She shook her head. "When you didn't bolt out of bed the first time Alix called you, I figured you needed the sleep."

"Hi, squirt." He sat in the chair nearest his niece.

She held out a sticky hand and offered him a piece of her pancake.

"I'll pass," he said with a grin.

Chelsie stood and walked over to the stove, returning with a covered plate. "I saved these for you." She poured him a cup of coffee and pushed the bottle of maple syrup towards him.

His mouth watered again. "Thanks."

"No problem."

Though they had agreed to talk, he decided to delay anything personal until later and tackled the subject of work instead. "I was wondering how Amanda took things when you told her you'd filed the restraining order against her ex." He had been too busy with his own caseload and filling in for Mrs. Baxter during the day to discuss every client with Chelsie.

She glanced up from her plate. "I didn't."

"How could you let a week go by without taking action?"

"Don't criticize before you know all the facts. Amanda wanted time to get settled before she filed any papers. Since her husband doesn't know where she is, she didn't think the delay would hurt."

"Didn't you tell her what a foolish, not to mention dangerous, attitude that is?" he asked.

Her skin turned ashen at the reminder and she placed her fork down with unsteady hands. "Of course. But you can't make someone move before they're ready. Some women never are," she murmured.

"It's not that I don't sympathize. You know I do. But how can she not want to go after the guy? He physically hurt her, for God's sake."

"Being a victim entails a lot more than just physical abuse. Sometimes the emotional ramifications are worse," she said in a shaky voice. "Some women just want to put the whole experience behind them as quickly as possible."

He sighed, placing a hand on her arm. "I didn't mean to sound judgmental, and I didn't mean to bring back old memories."

"I've lived with them for a long time, Griff. Don't go taking on any guilt." She stood and cleared Alix's high chair, then turned her attention to cleaning off the child.

Because she seemed to need the distraction, he didn't offer to do it for her. Instead, he collected the dishes from the table and placed them in the sink.

Chelsie unstrapped the little girl from the harness that held her in the chair and deposited her on the white ceramic tile floor. "Go play," she whispered in her ear.

Alix didn't need any more encouragement. She took off in the direction of her toys.

Once they were alone, he walked over and wrapped his arms around Chelsie's slender waist. He buried his face in the back of her neck, inhaling her feminine scent and recalling details of the time she'd spent in his arms.

"Griff, there is one thing I need to ask."

"Can't it wait?" He tangled his fingers in her hair and thought of the bed upstairs. Work was the last thing on his mind.

"I've already put this off too long," she said.

Apparently, he hadn't done as good a job as he'd planned last night, he thought wryly. She wasn't too exhausted for a long discussion and he sensed he'd have a difficult time deterring her. "What's up?"

"You'll have to take over Amanda's case from now on."

That request stunned him. Grasping her shoulders, he pivoted her body until she faced him, but she wouldn't meet his gaze. Her downcast eyes and the erratic tapping of her foot against the floor hinted at a serious problem. They'd been as close as two people could be. So why this sudden reticence to discuss something as impersonal as work?

"What's going on?" he asked.

She lifted her head and looked him in the eye.

"Why should I take that particular case?" he asked.

Chelsie could have said it was what the other woman wanted. She could have claimed Amanda's situation hit too close to her own. She could have blamed her already overloaded schedule. Any one of those excuses sounded valid and held enough truth to satisfy Griff, but as her partner—no, as her lover—he deserved the truth.

Regardless of the consequences, she had no intention of running out on him emotionally or otherwise. "Because there might be a conflict of . . ."

The shrill ring of the telephone cut her off midsentence.

Griff cast her an apologetic glance. Divine intervention, she thought with dismay. The one time she truly didn't want any interruptions, she got one anyway.

She placed a stalling hand on his arm. "Can we ignore it?" she asked.

He glanced over at the phone. "Work line. Who would be calling on a Sunday?"

I check in periodically. Call any time. A jittery feeling settled in the pit of her stomach.

"Amanda," Chelsie said, automatically. This wasn't the first time she'd been called on a weekend or in the middle of the night by a client or someone at the shelter. The timing couldn't be worse, but she'd never ignore someone who needed help. Especially Amanda.

The flutters in Chelsie's stomach turned into lead. "I've got it." She darted across the kitchen and grabbed the receiver. "Hello?"

Chelsie nodded at Griff, letting him know she'd been right. The hysterical woman rambled, but Chelsie caught the gist of the conversation and didn't like what she was hearing. "How could he find you?" she asked and listened in disbelief to Amanda's answer. "Just stay where you are. I'll meet you in"—Chelsie glanced at her watch—"less than twenty minutes."

Frustrated, she slammed the phone onto the receiver. Adrenaline should have kept her energy level up, but a deep weariness had settled inside her. Fighting her ex-husband would be a losing battle if she couldn't trust her client. She turned back to Griff. "Amanda had a confrontation with her husband. It seems she went home to pick up a few things."

"Why the hell would she do something like that?" He nearly exploded in anger. Chelsie didn't blame him. If the woman had gone home for something as stupid as extra clothing, Chelsie would throttle her.

She shook her head. "I don't know. She didn't

give me too many details. Look, I'll go and calm her down."

"Not alone, you won't."

She pivoted on her heels, furious that he had the audacity to bark orders and grateful he cared enough to try. One look at his drawn face and her anger ebbed. He leaned against a chair. His hand grasped the back of the seat with such force his knuckles turned white. She could fight his bossiness, but not his concern.

"I'll be fine. There's no alternative. You can't go to the shelter and someone has to stay with Alix." She walked over to him and smoothed the worry lines on his forehead with one finger. "Can I borrow your car?"

"It won't work."

"What?" The corners of her lips twitched in a knowing smile.

"Distracting me, though you always give it your best shot." He gently removed her hand, then reached over and grasped a set of keys off the counter. "I'll meet you at your apartment as soon as Mrs. Baxter gets here." He slapped the cold metal keys into her open palm and leaned close, brushing his warm lips over hers.

"With what? I'm taking your car. Don't worry. I'll meet you back here as soon as I'm finished." She could soothe Amanda, then leave her in competent hands.

"At least call me the minute you're through."

"Yes, sir. Anyone ever tell you you're bossy?"

A sad smile crossed his face. "My brother."

"I'm sorry," she whispered, wishing she could permanently ease his pain. But she knew from her own fragile emotions that he'd live with some variation of the hurt for the rest of his life.

He lifted his hands to her face and she savored the feel of his strong touch against her skin. "I love you." She spoke honestly, without thinking. She wrapped her arms around his neck, meeting him halfway for a kiss that melted her defenses. Though Chelsie felt safe in his arms, the kiss was anything but. All the passion, heat, and tangled emotions threatened to overwhelm her.

A sheen of perspiration coated his forehead. His breathing sounded labored. "You'd better get going," he murmured.

Chelsie smiled, finding it difficult to catch her own breath. " 'Bye."

It wasn't until she reached the shelter that she realized she had told Griff the truth. But not the truth that mattered most.

"You keep showing up unexpectedly and I'll have to charge you rent." Griff unlocked the storm door for Ryan.

Morning had turned into afternoon and then to early evening without a word from Chelsie. Griff understood her preoccupation with Amanda's plight and, as a lawyer, understood that emergencies arose even on weekends. But his concern grew with each passing minute.

Ryan chuckled and, as usual, brushed past Griff into the house. "I take it you won't be needing my baby-sitting services any longer?"

"Quit fishing for information. I haven't needed your services in months. Consider yourself greatly appreciated but now unemployed."

"Right. Miss Russell is filling in." Ryan paused to plant a kiss on Alix's cheek. She reciprocated with a wet one on his lips, causing him to chuckle. "Speaking of Chelsie . . ."

"I wasn't," Griff said. Thinking of her, definitely, but not sharing his personal thoughts, even with Ryan.

"I was. I did you a favor." Ryan held out a manila envelope.

Griff glanced at the distinctive packet. He'd seen the results of Ryan's investigations one too many times to be mistaken. "I thought I told you to leave her alone."

"Friends help friends." Ryan tossed the envelope onto the cocktail table. "Your decision," he said and turned to play with Alix.

Knowing he had to get rid of the information before Chelsie returned, Griff scowled at Ryan before swiping the offending envelope from the table. He walked straight upstairs and into his office, placing the file in the top drawer of his desk. He saw no reason to upset Chelsie by telling her that a private investigator, Ryan of all people, had looked into her past. He'd dump the file later, when he could eliminate it permanently.

Griff had no intention of reading any information Chelsie didn't disclose on her own. She'd indicated earlier that they had to talk, and he felt sure she would confide in him over time.

A lifetime, he realized with sudden clarity.

He'd known for a while that they couldn't continue an affair with a two-year-old child in the house. In his heart, he knew he wanted Chelsie forever. He just wished his mind, so cluttered with images of the past, would leave him alone. But Chelsie had helped him begin to heal.

She cared about *him*, not what he could give her, buy her, or do for her. No woman had given him that gift before. For that reason alone, he trusted her enough to attempt to build a future.

He glanced at his watch. What the hell was taking her so long?

"Hey, Ryan." Griff bounded back downstairs and imposed on his long-time friend one more time.

"So you went home for your son's favorite stuffed animal." Chelsie sat with Amanda in one of the few empty rooms of the shelter.

Posters cluttered the beige walls in an attempt to brighten what should have been a morose and depressing atmosphere. Anyone who made this place a pit stop had left severe problems outside these walls, but many brought children along with them. And where there were children, there was hope.

"Stupid, huh? It's just that he hasn't slept since we got here over a week ago."

Chelsie clasped her hands together while attempting to formulate a reasonable response, one that didn't take emotion into account. "You're a good mother, Amanda. But some risks are just too great. You gambled with this one."

The other woman bent her head, causing her dark hair to fall forward and obscure her face from view.

"Jeff was home. Did he hurt you?"

"No. Just begged me to come back."

"And?"

"I said I'd think about it. Just to bide time," she

quickly added. "After we talked, I grabbed the animal and left fast."

Chelsie wasn't reassured. "He let you walk out of there?"

Amanda nodded. Chelsie remained silent. From past experience with other clients, and from her married days, Chelsie knew Jeffrey's lack of pressure meant he had an alternate plan.

"Amanda, if you're still serious about divorcing him, then we've got to get moving. I have statements from your friends and relatives. I've got pictures of the bruises the last time he hit you. Now it's time for legal action. I want a restraining order taken out as soon as possible. And I want you to seriously consider pressing charges. Okay?"

"He'll be furious."

"Yes. But he doesn't know where you are, so you're safe. Unless . . ."

"I didn't say a word. I swear."

Chelsie breathed a sigh of relief. "All right. I'll handle things. Just don't do anything like that again. Don't go home. Don't go near his office. Don't get in touch with him at all."

"You're sure about all this?" Amanda lifted her head. Sad, dark eyes looked to Chelsie for reassurance.

"You're the one who has to be certain." Chelsie grasped the other woman's shoulders. "But if you're asking my opinion, then yes, press charges. Stand up for yourself and your child. I didn't. As a result, you're in this position now, and I'll never have the future I want. I'd hate to see the pattern repeat itself."

Tears shimmered in the other woman's eyes, but she nodded her assent.

"Good. I'll be in touch."

Chelsie left Amanda behind and instead of going to Griff's, she headed for home. Shutting the door to her apartment, she turned the lock firmly behind her. She needed a reality check before taking her next step.

Once in the living room, she flicked on the overhead lights. The crystal animals sat in a pile on the floor where Alix had left them. Chelsie knelt down and picked one up, fingering the small bear with a delicate hand. What would it feel like to have a child you loved so much you would risk your life to retrieve a simple toy? Alix immediately came to mind. Faced with such a decision, Chelsie knew she'd do anything to keep that dimpled smile on the little girl's face. She'd do anything to make the child's uncle happy, even if it meant sacrificing her own desires.

A tear dripped down her cheek and she caught it with her sleeve. *How would she ever let them go?* Clutching the bear in her fist, she brought the animal close to her heart.

By becoming a part of Griff and Alix's life, she had set herself up for the heartache she'd avoided for years by pulling away from her sister, her only real family member who cared. Not for the first time, Chelsie wished she'd had the courage to take this risk sooner, so she and Shannon would have had more time. She didn't miss the irony. Revealing the truth to her sister would have brought them back together, while telling Griff everything would drive them apart.

Chelsie hadn't played this smart. She had gotten too close, too involved with a man who wanted more children, and too involved with her niece, the child she loved like the daughter she'd never have.

When she finally faced what she had done, she

accepted the fact that she'd acted on instinct. Alone and afraid, she had saved herself without thought to those who would come after her. She couldn't change her own actions, but she'd attempted to atone ever since. Although she'd volunteered, counseled, and represented women who needed her, the sin of being selfish haunted her even today. Wasn't Amanda proof?

It was enough. Didn't she deserve a chance at happiness? Maybe Griff would understand and accept. A big maybe, she knew. If not, at least she'd taken a step towards regaining her life.

She glanced around the apartment and knew she couldn't remain here any longer. Since Griff and Alix, this sterile environment no longer suited her.

A loud knock startled her out of her reverie. Maybe this was her chance. Griff might not have a car, but he hadn't let it keep him away. Knowing him, he'd hijacked Ryan and brought Alix along.

She ran to the door, fumbling with the lock and swinging it open as she spoke. "Griff . . ." Her smile froze and so did her heart.

"Hi, Chelsie. It's been a long time."

"Jeff." Her voice sounded hoarse, strange even to her own ears. Five years dissolved as if they'd never been, but she refused to show a hint of fear. Disregarding the blood that surged to her head and her suddenly damp palms, she glared at her ex-husband.

"You remember." He pushed her aside, entering her apartment without invitation.

How had he gotten past the doorman? *I latched onto a large party, and if I could do that, so could anyone.* Her safe haven didn't feel safe anymore. Griff had warned her. Somehow, she didn't think he'd take too much pleasure in being right this time.

"You're looking well." Jeff's eyes traveled the length of her body. Though fully clothed, she felt as if he'd stripped her bare with his gaze. A strong wave of nausea washed over her and she clamped down on the nerves and memories that churned her stomach.

Jeff stood half a room away. He hadn't changed. His slick blond hair had that just-styled appearance. Not a hint of razor stubble marred his chiseled features. He wore his trademark navy blue suit with a maroon tie. He hardly looked the abusive type, but then, there was no such thing. Appearances meant little. In Jeff Sutton's case, latent violence seethed beneath the conservative facade. How he'd managed to bury that side of his nature for the first year of their marriage still amazed her.

Chelsie hung onto her composure by a slender thread. "I'm sure you didn't come to exchange pleasantries." She tried to swallow, but her mouth was too dry. She walked to the window, away from her ex-husband. "How did you find me?"

He smiled and lowered himself onto her couch, stretching his long legs in front of him. "How about a drink for an ex-husband?"

"How about an answer?"

"Finding you was easy. I followed you after your meeting with my present wife. Amanda never knew I tailed her from our home. Her meeting with you was a definite surprise—although you never did know when to mind your own business." He flicked a spot of lint off his dark suit.

Chelsie wasn't fooled by his bland tone and seeming lack of interest. "She hired my firm. That makes it my business."

He shook his head in a patronizing manner that indicated he thought she was sadly mistaken. "Maybe after we're through *talking,* you won't be so quick to step into other people's lives."

"Is that a threat?"

His casual smile didn't fool her. "I don't threaten, you know that."

No, he lashed out.

"I just want to talk, Chels."

"We have nothing left to say."

Jeff shook his head. "Actually that's not true. Someone's been digging into our affairs, and it's become a damned nuisance."

She narrowed her gaze. "What do you mean?"

"I let you go without a fight because you promised no one would ever know. I gave you that divorce as a parting gift, but did you really think I could risk not covering myself? I have a career that means everything to me. If someone found out you were careless enough to fall down the stairs and I let it happen . . ."

"You mean if someone found out you *pushed me.*"

With no warning, he sprang up from the couch. She'd pushed him too far. Chelsie bit her lower lip and gauged the distance to the door. Jeff blocked any escape.

He walked towards her, his stride deceptively lazy. "I have a friend in hospital records, and someone's been snooping." Griff, Chelsie wondered? Had he hired someone to dig for information for Amanda? If so, what did he know?

Jeff grabbed her arm, yanking her back to face

him. "Make sure it doesn't happen again. Have your boyfriend back off and tell my wife to come home."

She wouldn't allow him to see how badly he rattled her, and she inhaled deep. His cologne hadn't changed either. The sweet smell almost made her gag. She stepped backwards and her heel hit the wall. She'd trapped herself, and the feeling of *déjà vu* wasn't particularly comforting.

He lifted one hand and ran a finger down the length of her cheek. The feel of his hands on her skin repulsed her. She jerked her head back and came into hard contact with the wall. She closed her eyes against the dizziness, then opened them again. Her skull ached from the blow. "Get out," she said through clenched teeth.

She lifted her right leg, bringing her foot down on his. Unfortunately, sneakers didn't cause much pain. His larger physical size gave him an advantage, one she had hoped to overcome.

He slid his large hand around the back of her neck until his fingers tangled in her hair. "Be nice to me, Chelsie," he whispered, his head bent close to hers. With his free hand, he ran his thumb over her lower lip. He watched her closely as he brought that same finger to his mouth.

She shuddered despite her resolve.

"Let's just call this a settlement meeting about Amanda's case," he said.

"There's nothing to settle. Your wife wants out."

He tightened his grip and his fingers dug into her scalp. "I won't let her go as easily as I let you."

Though Chelsie forced a laugh, her voice rose in direct proportion to her growing sense of panic. "You didn't *let* me do anything. It was a quick di-

vorce or jail. You knew that. This time, there are no
options. You'll get both."

He shook his head and leaned closer. "This time
I have a son," he said in a loud, clear voice. His
forceful tone left no doubt that he intended to get
his way, regardless of the means. To make his point,
he pulled back on her hair.

Though she suppressed a groan, Chelsie no
longer cared about the physical pain. Lashing out
at the person she had allowed to ruin her life over-
rode all sense of caution. "You had one last time,
too," she spat at him.

His eyes darkened in fury. As he yanked her backwards, her head hit the wall again. Tears sprang to
her eyes. She bit her lip but refused to utter a sound.
Her helplessness rose like bile in her throat. The
past five years closed in on her, suffocating her worse
than Jeff's proximity.

Suddenly, Chelsie couldn't take any more. She
wanted to live again. She wanted to be free.

ELEVEN

Griff stepped out of the elevator. Voices carried down the corridor leading to Chelsie's apartment. City living was much different than suburban life, he mused, thinking of his quiet home.

When he reached her partially open door, he realized one of the voices belonged to Chelsie. The words stopped him cold and he couldn't help but overhear.

"This time I have a son."

"You had one last time, too." Silence punctuated her statement. "You killed my baby." Her voice raised in near hysteria. "I'll be damned if I'll let you do it to Amanda." She was sobbing now, and the heartwrenching sounds made Griff move. He burst into the apartment.

Her back was pressed against the wall. Tears streamed down her cheeks. The man Griff assumed was Jeffrey Sutton stood beside her. He raised one hand and Griff realized the other held Chelsie against her will. He cursed the time he'd spent outside her apartment.

"Chelsie." She jerked her head towards the sound of his voice, wincing as she did so. Her ex-husband turned to see who had interrupted. Griff took one step forward, but Chelsie moved faster. Taking advantage of the opportunity, she smashed her hand against the back of the other man's head. He staggered away from her with a loud moan.

She looked down at her hand in stunned silence. Griff watched as one of her crystal treasures fell from her fingers. She followed, sliding to the floor in relief.

Griff grabbed the man by the back of his suit collar, thrusting him up against the same wall where he'd cornered Chelsie. Rage filled him. This man had laid his hands on Chelsie again. Blood rushed to his head and pounded in his veins. So easy, he thought. He could kill Jeffrey Sutton without a second thought.

"How does it feel to be cornered?" Griff asked.

The other man remained silent.

"You're not so brave against someone your own size." Griff raised his fist. "One good blow could do a lot of damage. Then again, jail could do a lot more."

The man turned white beneath an obviously fake tan.

"Griff, don't." Chelsie's low voice penetrated the throbbing anger that heated his body.

"Press charges, Chelsie."

Her gaze swung back and forth between the two men, but she remained silent. Griff knew she might be in shock. Dealing with the police could come later. She no longer had to face Jeffrey Sutton alone.

He turned to the man Chelsie had once called her husband. "You're a lawyer, so understand this. From now on, you'd better act like a restraining order has already been issued. Stay the hell away from Chelsie *and* Amanda."

Chelsie emitted a startled cry. Griff turned towards her, unwittingly loosening his hold on the man he'd had pinned to the wall. Jeff darted around Griff and out the door without looking back.

Chelsie ran straight into his arms. Half an hour passed in which Griff did nothing but hold on tight. When the adrenaline pumping through his veins subsided, concern for Chelsie filled the void. The questions came next.

"I take back every rotten thing I ever thought about those animals," he said.

"They did come in useful." She leaned her head against his shoulder before pulling away and wrapping her arms around her legs. Her chin rested on her knees and she gazed at him from beneath thick lashes. She appeared pale, but composed. If he'd arrived any later, if her ex-husband had seriously hurt her . . .

"He didn't hurt me. Not really," she said, rubbing her scalp. Her insight into his private thoughts didn't surprise him. "But . . ."

"What?"

"This is going to sound ridiculous." She averted her gaze.

"Let me be the judge of that. What's on your mind?"

"He touched me." Her hand went to her cheek. "As if he still had the right."

Griff drew a steadying breath. "He didn't . . ." Griff couldn't finish the thought.

She shook her head. "But this place has always been untouched by him. And being here, I could pretend it never happened, but now I feel so violated."

"It's not ridiculous." Grasping her hand, he

squeezed once for reassurance before pulling her to her feet. "And I have the perfect solution."

Menial tasks like pouring bath water and finding towels helped him keep his mind off everything he'd overheard. Everything he'd like to forget.

Settled in a warm bubble bath, Chelsie looked up at Griff and smiled. The serene expression did more than anything else to assure him that her ex-husband's damage had been minimal.

"I stood up to him, didn't I?" she asked.

"Yeah. You did." Not enough, since he'd like to see the bastard behind bars, but she'd made a start. He'd never been so proud and so damned frightened in his entire life. This woman made him feel things that were foreign to him. Feelings that went beyond sexual and bordered on love. But borders changed on a whim. His feelings for Chelsie were cemented on a more solid foundation. Not that he discounted the sexual attraction. He couldn't. The only reason he was able to sit on the edge of the tub and maintain a coherent conversation was because bubbles surrounded her otherwise naked body.

She lifted a handful of soap and blew in his direction. She'd caught him drifting. "This whole experience has me rattled, too," he said.

"How did you make the connection between me and Amanda?" She lowered her lashes in embarrassment.

"I overheard." *This time, I have a son. You had one last time, too.* Forgetting wasn't an option for either of them.

"I'm sorry. I wanted to tell you about Jeff and how Amanda looked me up on purpose, but the words wouldn't come."

They had now because circumstances had forced her to speak. If she'd had her way, she'd probably have maintained her silence, leaving him in the dark.

She shrugged. "Now you know. But there's more."

Griff remained silent, sensing any word from him might cause her to clam up once again. He needed the truth. All of it.

"No matter what you think of me after this, there's something you have to know."

He gazed at her face. The flush that covered her cheeks might have been from the heat of the bath, but he sensed something more. "What?"

"I love you," she whispered. "I wasn't lying this morning. I love you both, you and Alix. I think I have almost from the very beginning." She smiled. "Despite the tragedy that brought you two together, you're a lucky man. Family is a precious gift. And you've both given me so much."

No more than she had given them, which made this all the more difficult. "Chelsie, I . . ." A soft but soapy finger over his lips cut him off.

"Don't. Just listen."

He nodded and she withdrew her hand. His tongue swiped over his lips, leaving the bitter taste of soap in its wake. He grimaced and wiped his mouth with the back of his sleeve.

She chuckled aloud, but there was no light dancing in her eyes. He missed her gentle touch, and the chill that seeped around him despite the heat in the bathroom frightened him more than he cared to admit.

"You already know I can't handle Amanda's case because she's married to my ex-husband. For me to take the case would be a definite conflict of interest and would jeopardize her right to fair representation."

The matter-of-fact way she laid out the facts, the way she tried to appear composed and unaffected, was destroyed by the sheen of tears in her dark eyes. Griff thought of the bruises on Amanda's arms and Jeff Sutton's hard grip on Chelsie today. His gaze dropped to her white skin and he clenched his jaw.

"I'll handle it." With pleasure, he thought.

"Fairly?"

"Give me some credit. I might like to kill the bastard, but in a court of law, I'll be fair."

She nodded. "Good. I hope you'll apply that same concept to what I have to say next, because this story isn't your usual marriage, divorce, unhappily ever after."

He glanced towards the tub and realized she'd begun to shiver, though she was too engrossed in thought to even notice. Reaching for the yellow robe on the back of the door, he held it out. "Should I give you a few minutes?"

"At this point, I think modesty is a little late, don't you?"

As she stood, Griff looked away. He couldn't pinpoint the exact source of his anxiety, but he couldn't discount the nagging feelings, either. Sexual desire would only complicate things. When he glanced back, she was lifting the damp ends of her hair from beneath the collar of her robe.

He followed her into the living room, joining her on the couch. Entwining her slender fingers in his grasp, he said, "Talk to me."

She sucked in a gulp of air and nodded. "When they admitted me to the hospital that night five years ago, the nurse who helped me into those awful dressing gowns noticed the bruises on my arms. After that, it wasn't difficult to keep my husband away. The police sent a detective to take a statement. She said she'd come back the next day for me to sign an official version."

"Sounds like standard procedure so far." He hoped his casual acceptance, his nonchalant attitude would help her get through whatever she had to say.

"So far," she agreed. "I was pregnant. I'd known for a while, but we'd been growing apart instead of together. I planned to tell him after the cocktail party that night. My big surprise," she said with more than a touch of bitterness.

"What . . ."

"Please, this is hard enough. Just let me get through it, okay?" Her eyes filled with unshed tears, wrenching at his heart.

"Okay."

"Within a few hours of being admitted, I started having these awful cramps." Her hand went to her stomach, covering her abdomen. She stared straight ahead, as if a mere glance in his direction would cause her to fall apart.

Without warning or invitation, a vision of Chelsie, pregnant with his child, rose in his mind. The image filled the empty spaces he hadn't even realized were inside him.

"I lost the baby." Tears dripped down her face and she swiped at them with the back of one hand. "Then the doctors had no problem taking x rays and doing all sorts of tests. Turns out I had a severe concussion, too. They all understood when I told them I didn't want Jeff to know about the baby. It wouldn't serve any purpose except to enrage an already demented man."

"I'm sorry." He moved closer, sliding towards her end of the couch.

"Don't." She shook her head, halting his approach. "This is where the story gets messy."

"Take your time." He realized they had to do this her way.

"At the time, I needed to get away from him. Far away from his temper, his influence, and the reminders. Jeff was determined to be on the partnership track at one of the largest firms in the city of Boston. Any hint of a scandal, any inkling that he had a violent nature or beat his wife would destroy his career. I knew that." She exhaled a shaky breath. "So I threatened him. Fly down to some Caribbean island and get a quick divorce, or I would sign that statement and press charges. The hospital had documentation. He had no choice."

As five long years of suppressed memories came spewing forth, her voice and demeanor grew more confident. A stronger woman emerged with each revelation, one who wasn't afraid of the truth. Despite the pain of resurrecting the past, Griff noticed a definite lifting of Chelsie's spirits. He sensed the change, even if she didn't.

"You bribed him," he said. Until her response, he hadn't been aware of speaking aloud.

"Yes. I'm not proud of it, but at the time, I thought it was best. I was alone. My parents were never the supportive types. They wouldn't have approved of the scandal this could have created. I couldn't face my sister. She'd just gotten married to a wonderful man. I didn't think she'd understand, and I couldn't bear to watch."

Comprehension came to him in a flash of insight, so strong he wondered why he hadn't realized it sooner. Chelsie wasn't the type to ignore family, to avoid a little girl. Not without strong personal reasons. "So that's why you never visited, never spent time with Jared and Shannon."

She nodded slowly and two teardrops coursed down her cheeks. "What can I say? I know now I was wrong . . . but she's gone."

Along with his brother. At least he'd had a semblance of closure with his sibling. "But I'm not. You can talk to me. I won't judge you."

"You don't have to. I've spent the last five years doing just that. My entire career has been spent making up for thinking of myself first. When I let Jeff off the hook, I freed him to abuse some other woman. At the time, I wasn't thinking that clearly. Sure, I thought about my own future, but not about anyone else. Each case I took that involved an abused woman, I told myself that I was making a difference."

"You did."

She twirled a strand of hair around one finger. "But I refused to allow myself to think about what Jeff did with his life after the divorce. Probably because deep down I knew."

"You aren't responsible for anyone but yourself."

"Funny you should mention that." Her bitter laugh sounded too harsh. "In the end, I didn't do such a hot job in that area, either."

"What do you mean?"

She sighed, placing her head in her hands. When

she spoke, he could barely hear. "There were complications from the miscarriage. They gave me antibiotics when I left the hospital. I was supposed to finish the prescription and come back in to be checked. I finished the bottle, but I never went for the follow-up exam. I wanted to bury myself so deep in work that I never had time to think about Jeff Sutton, my failed marriage, or lost baby ever again." She lifted her head. Tears streamed down her face. She let them fall. "I just wanted to forget the past, not destroy the future."

He laid a hand over hers, startled by how cold her skin felt against his. "What happened?"

"A year went by. By the time I got around to that checkup, I had severe pelvic inflammatory disease. There was scarring. I can never have children of my own."

"I'm sorry," he murmured.

He drew her into his arms, whispered all the right words, and caressed her until she seemed to relax, wishing he could do the same. Unfortunately, his tension had just begun.

He had fallen in love with Chelsie because she wanted nothing from him. Because she seemed to care for him unconditionally. Because unlike Deidre and his mother, Chelsie wanted Griff the man, not what he could give her. Or so he had thought.

She said she loved both him and Alix. Under ordinary circumstances, those would be the exact words he would want to hear from any woman he contemplated spending the rest of his life with. Though Alix was her niece and Chelsie would always play a role in her life, Griff had custody. Alix was a part of his life on a daily basis. Forever. The woman he loved had to love her, too. Had to want a little girl in her life.

But Chelsie couldn't have children. And here he was, a man with a child, a ready-made family she could call her own. He couldn't deny that the cynic in him lived on, created by women who'd used and betrayed him in the past. Had Chelsie fallen in love with the notion of family that he and Alix offered?

She'd said as much herself. *Family is a precious gift. You've both given me so much.* He didn't believe Chelsie would deliberately use them to achieve something she couldn't have on her own. But she hadn't told him the facts up front, not even after they'd made love. Why not? Unless she, too, wanted something from him and was afraid of losing it by revealing all. Consciously or unconsciously, the truth remained, and so did his doubts.

"I love you," she murmured.

Though he held her in his arms and brushed a kiss against her temple, Griff remained silent.

A few uncomfortable minutes later, he pulled away and stood.

"Griff?"

"I've got to get back to Alix."

She blinked, pain flashing in her eyes for a millisecond before her expression changed to one of acceptance. Her mind had obviously assessed and discounted the truth of his statement. She knew as well as he did that Alix was well cared for in his absence. There was no rush, except for his sudden need to be alone.

The wounded look passed so quickly, he thought he'd been mistaken. The twisting in his gut told him otherwise. Before she banked the emotion, her vulnerability had shown plainly on her face. "Will you be all right?" he asked.

She pulled the lapels of her robe together, keeping her hands at her throat. "Of course."

The strain between them, the distance that hadn't been there earlier, settled on his shoulders. He'd caused the tension. He could easily rectify matters. Two steps forward, a touch, and Chelsie would be in his arms.

She brushed past him to open the door. The soft scent of the bubble bath lingered in the air. Just two steps. It might as well have been two miles. He laid a hand on her cheek.

" 'Bye, Griff." Despite her firm tone, he caught the sheen of moisture in her eyes and the way she'd locked her jaw to keep any emotions from showing on her face.

He swallowed hard. "I just need some time."

She shrugged. He hadn't taken half a step into the hallway when the door shut behind him. He waited until he heard the turning of the dead bolt and the rattle of the chain on the door. The sounds of Chelsie closing him out of her life. Only then did he head for the bank of elevators, alone.

Coming to work hadn't been easy. Trying to deal with Griff had been even more of a trial. Looking at him hurt. Being in the same room but not being close to him hurt even more.

Every day business between them suffered as a result. Still, they owed their clients, including Amanda, their best. "Just make sure the judge grants the restraining order immediately," Chelsie said. "I'll handle things here."

"No problem." Griff picked up a stack of files and placed them in his briefcase without once meeting her gaze.

She pushed aside the waves of nausea and anxiety and kept herself busy instead. A few more minutes and she'd be alone. No more pretense, no more pretending it didn't hurt.

Stepping outside his office, she poured two cups of coffee from the pot in the reception area before returning to face him. "Here. It's decaf."

He looked up and graced her with a scowl, the first true sign of recognition he'd given her all morning. "You're wound so tight you'll explode at the slightest problem," she explained. "Besides, I won't watch you overdose on caffeine."

He grunted in response. Chelsie sighed. Ignoring the real problem wouldn't solve anything, but she'd promised herself she'd try. For his sake, she had to do her best. After all, she understood. He needed time, so she'd give him time. Even if it turned out to be forever.

"You'd better get going or you'll be late." She handed him Amanda Sutton's case file.

"Thanks." Without glancing in her direction, he stuffed the papers in his briefcase and walked out.

With her heart lodged somewhere in her throat, Chelsie watched him go. Though she had expected this reaction, she couldn't say his attitude didn't hurt. But she'd lived without him before, and she would do so again.

Even as she'd realized that Griff's silence didn't bode well for their relationship, she finally felt a measure of self-worth that had nothing to do with her status as an attorney. Chelsie now accepted her mistakes. She had atoned for them as best as she knew how.

She would learn to live without children of her own, without hiding in a crystal palace that mocked her infertility and represented her poor judgment. If anything, that apartment now reminded her of Alix and the joy children could bring anywhere, even a place they weren't meant to be.

She had Griff to thank for her new attitude. Unfortunately, he didn't seem to want to be a part of her life. When she let herself feel, the pain was almost unbearable. She knew she would have to deal with that, but first she needed to reestablish one other important relationship in her life. After flipping through her calendar, she placed a call to her parents at their vacation home in Florida. Minutes later, she'd booked a flight.

She spent the next few hours scrambling to organize her caseload, cram as much as she could into the coming week, and free up her weekend.

She glanced around her cluttered desk, but piles of manila folders blocked any productive search. "Where would I put those files?" she muttered.

If she managed to interview a few extra potential witnesses this week and postponed a messy divorce that was destined to carry on forever anyway, she could take three days off with no problem. But not if the expert witness file didn't turn up sometime soon.

After ransacking her office and badgering their secretary, Chelsie went to Griff's office, hoping he'd borrowed the list for Amanda's case. She silently blessed him for his share-with-your-partner policy. The man didn't care if she went through his desk, his books, or his papers, as long as she returned things so he could find them later.

As her partner, he had turned out to be great. As her lover . . . she shook her head, refusing to travel that path until she had time alone to think things through.

Unlike Chelsie, Griff kept the top of his desk meticulously clean, so she knew immediately she'd have to search the drawers. She opened the top one, hoping she wouldn't have to search every file cabinet in the office.

She had no idea what order the files were in, so she flipped from the beginning. "What the hell?" The header on one contained her name in bold type and she withdrew a sheaf of papers.

She sifted through the assorted documents, sinking into his chair mid-way through. "Thorough background check, driving record, marriage license, divorce decree, hospital records, documentation of miscarriage and nurses' notations of possible spousal abuse," she read aloud.

Chelsie had discounted her ex-husband's words, but obviously Jeff had been right. Someone had been digging into her past. The list of documents went on and on. Not a single aspect of her life had been untouched or considered sacred.

She pressed the folder to her chest, feeling well and truly violated by the man she'd given her heart.

"Chelsie," Griff called out, striding into his office. "Gloria said you're looking for the list. I must have stuffed it into . . . What's wrong?"

She raised her head and looked at him. "You ought to lock up private documents, or at least not be so liberal about sharing your office." She tossed the file onto his empty desk, watching as the papers scattered across the dark wood. "Anything you wanted to know, all you had to do was ask. I never once lied to you. Omitted facts, maybe, but I never lied."

Slowly, he lowered his briefcase into the nearest chair. His expression revealed nothing. "Anything I learned, I wanted to hear from you first."

"So explain this." She jerked her hands towards the documents, lifting one in her hand.

"A concerned friend."

"Ryan," she muttered.

He nodded. "But not my idea."

"So you didn't ask your best friend to dig up all the dirt on my sordid past?"

A muscle twitched in his cheek. "That hurts, Chelsie. I thought you knew me better than that. I turned down an opportunity to have Ryan investigate before we became partners."

"So you had an attack of morality. But that didn't stop you from reading the information when you had the chance." Given the curiosity inherent in human nature, Chelsie wouldn't be surprised if he had. She also wouldn't blame him. He'd gone against his initial instincts.

Despite her mistake in suing for custody on her parents' behalf, he'd taken her into his home and practically shared custody of Alix. With her family's track record and his niece's welfare at stake, Griff had a right to delve as deeply as he wanted into her life.

"It sure as hell did." His dark eyes narrowed. Anger emanated from the arrogant tilt of his head to the hand he slammed against the desk. "Think about it."

She paused. When she tried to view yesterday's

revelations from an unbiased perspective, she had no choice but to believe him. If he had known of her infertility, the information wouldn't have thrown him as it had. There would have been no reason for him to take off or for him to need time on his own. Certainly, he would have had an opportunity to anticipate how to respond should she choose to confide in him. On the other hand, if he hadn't known, he'd be shocked and react accordingly. And he had.

Only one question remained. How did Griff feel about her now? She'd laid her heart out for him, and he hadn't accepted her love. But he hadn't rejected it either.

"And now that you know everything?" she asked, her eyes never leaving his.

Griff wasn't surprised that she'd all but asked his intentions. It was only a matter of time. As an attorney, he'd seen her question, cross-examine, and win the toughest cases. Only in her personal life had she seemed fragile, but that fragility cracked yesterday. She'd grown stronger since. When she'd admitted her past, she had faced her own demons. After that, cornering Griff about his feelings couldn't be too tough.

He sat on the corner of his desk, watching as she swiveled her chair back and forth.

"I'm not pressuring you for an answer. I'm just curious about what's going through your mind," she said.

He decided on honesty. "Remember I told you I'd been engaged?"

She nodded. "You're still in love with her?" Her voice nearly cracked under the strain of asking such a potentially devastating question.

"I don't think I ever was. I think she fulfilled certain expectations," he admitted, thinking of his self-ish ex-fiancée.

"Such as?"

"She left me when things got rough. She wanted my six-figure salary and the perks that came along with the partnership. She wanted what I could give her, but she never wanted me."

"Or Alix," Chelsie murmured.

"Exactly. You, on the other hand, claim to want both."

She narrowed her eyes and Griff could almost see her analytical mind sifting through the information. It was only a matter of time before she figured things out on her own. Griff waited.

"So the question is do I want you, or do I want what you can give me—what I can't have on my own?" She clenched her fists, apparently forgetting she still held the documents. The papers crumpled under the strain. "Is that an accurate assessment of what you're thinking?" she asked.

He bit down on the inside of his cheek. "Yes."

She nodded. "And here I thought your greatest concern would be that I couldn't give you children of your own. Tell me, is that also a problem for you, counselor?"

"No."

"Right." She surged to her feet, anger and hurt more than evident in her dark eyes. "Every man wants his own flesh and blood, Griff. Don't kid yourself or me. Somewhere down the line, you'd resent me because I couldn't give you a child of your own."

"Whatever put that idea in your head?"

She shrugged. "It doesn't matter. I only asked because I was curious."

He couldn't believe she thought so little of him. Could she truly think he'd only want her if she could bear his children? "You're wrong, Chelsie. It matters very much."

"Not really." She collected the scattered papers on the desk and shuffled them into a neat stack. "If you could even think that I'd use you, that all I want from you is what you could give me, then we never had much between us anyway."

"You don't believe that."

She shook her head and offered him a sad smile. "No. But obviously you do."

After placing the papers down, she rounded the corner of the desk and came up beside him. She placed a warm hand against his cheek. "I know you've lost a lot in your life. You're tough because you had to be. But if you continue to expect so little from people, that's exactly what you'll get in return."

"That's not what this is about."

"Isn't it? Your mother left you. Your ex-fiancée did the same. They both wanted something you couldn't give them. When they left, you were able to say, 'See, all women are alike.'" She paused to catch her breath. "When you realized I wasn't running anywhere, you got so damned scared you had to push me away. You're afraid to trust that I mean what I say, so you come up with the excuse that I'm just like them—I don't love you, I love what you can give me."

In an effort to get what she wanted and remain with Alix, *had* Chelsie convinced herself she loved him, too? Knowing her as he did, the thought was absurd. And yet . . .

He could never be sure. "Don't you?" The words escaped before he could stop them.

Her eyes opened wide. "No," she whispered.

The tears welling in the brown depths told him in no uncertain terms he'd pushed her too far. He'd hurt her in a fundamental way, and she deserved better. He reached out to her, but she stepped back to avoid his touch.

"I love Alix, and not just because she's my sister's child. I can't deny that and I wouldn't want to." She walked towards the door, head held high. "I trust this morning's hearing went well?"

All business. Perhaps that was just as well. Though her words stayed with him, he couldn't help wondering which one of them was suffering from delusions, Chelsie or himself. "Restraining order's right here," he said, patting his briefcase. "Jeff's being served as we speak." He met her gaze. "He'd be a fool to go near you now."

She nodded. "Anyway, I'll be out of town visiting my parents at the end of the week."

"Since when?"

"Like I told you. Family's important. I cleared my calendar and you don't need me." She cleared her throat, an obvious ruse to cover her shaken emotions. "I've got to set up appointments with those expert witnesses in the next few days."

He nodded. "The file is here." He pulled the folder from inside his briefcase.

She accepted it, careful to avoid his touch. He mentally acknowledged the pain, but refused to let it show. "I'll let you get to it, then. See you at dinner?"

She hesitated, staring at a point over his shoulder

when she finally answered. "I have too much work to do if I want to leave Friday."

He recognized her excuse for what it was. "Fine." Considering he'd cut her loose, what else could he say?

TWELVE

The humming of the machine as it copied and collated couldn't drum out the warm and tempting sounds from downstairs. A clatter of pots signaled dinner time, footsteps spoke of a home lived in and filled with love, and Alix's shrieks of laughter wouldn't be denied. Chelsie was forced to endure.

She tried to focus on the documents spread out on her desk, but the words blurred, memories of times she'd been a part of the family unit downstairs taking their place. She imagined Griff's gruff voice, huskier after they'd made love; his touch on her skin in places that belonged to him alone; his welcoming and often seductive smile. Chelsie had experienced each for the last time. Even knowing she had anticipated this back when Griff had proposed their partnership didn't make things bearable now.

A clatter, a thud, and the unmistakable sound of a child's cries rose towards her. Chelsie gripped the arms of her chair and jumped up from her seat before reminding herself that Griff was there. He was Alix's permanent guardian. Chelsie was a relative, a welcome *guest* in their home, but on a night like this, merely a partner who belonged upstairs . . . or didn't belong at all. She tiptoed to the bottom of the stairs to assure herself both Griff and Alix were okay, then collected her documents and headed for home. Changes were long overdue, Chelsie knew, and the time had come to make them.

Chelsie brought her suitcase with her to work on Friday. After an early meeting, she planned on taking a taxi to the airport. The morning was a disaster from the minute she awoke late because she'd forgotten to set her alarm clock for the right time.

She dressed in a hurry, wondering how she would survive the day. The beginning of the week had shown her how difficult life would be if she and Griff continued working together. They barely spoke. When they did, the strain from their personal lives insinuated itself into their partnership. Chelsie continued to depart from her previous routine of going downstairs for dinner. After her initial refusal on Monday, Griff hadn't asked again. She stopped working late at the office. As a result, her small living room now resembled a cluttered study.

She'd made a special effort to spend time with Alix while Griff was in court or working upstairs, but inevitably, dinner time came before she'd left for the day. The familiar sounds drifted upstairs, taunting her with what she'd almost had and lost. More than once, she wondered if Griff was right. Did she love what he could give her?

The answer was always the same. Yes. How could she not? Although she couldn't separate Griff and Alix, she felt certain she loved the man apart from the child. She loved his depth of caring, his ability to laugh, his skills as a lawyer. She loved arguing with him over a case and agreeing with him on strategy. She loved his ability to parent and adapt to any situation. Whether or not he had brought a child with him, Chelsie would have fallen hard.

But the fact remained that he had. That Alix shared her blood, too, didn't matter. Legally, the little girl lived with Griff. Until he believed he meant more to her than the package, he would never commit to an *us*. He would continue to wonder whether he could trust Chelsie's feelings. Though there was nothing she could do to change that, she didn't have to put herself through the pain.

An hour later, Chelsie shook hands with the man who had agreed to testify in an upcoming case and led him to the door. She glanced at her watch and realized she had fifteen minutes to spare before leaving for the airport. Drawing on all the reserve energy she had, she knocked once and entered Griff's office.

He sat behind his large mahogany desk, looking formidable and imposing.

"Morning," she said.

"How are you?"

"Fine." She wiped her palms on her skirt.

"About ready for your trip?"

She nodded. "May I?" She pointed to the couch. When he nodded, she lowered herself onto a cushion and motioned for him to join her.

He did, seating himself beside her. His thigh brushed hers. The familiar smell of his cologne warmed her and she closed her eyes, allowing herself a brief journey into the recent past before she opened them again. "Things weren't all bad, were they?"

He shook his head. "After you got over the shock of agreeing to help out, I'd have to say things went fairly well."

"Fairly?" She nudged him in the ribs with her elbow and he gave an obligatory grunt. "I was one heck of a baby-sitter."

He chuckled, letting her know he agreed. "What do you mean, *were?*" he asked, his voice sobering.

"This isn't going to work, is it?"

He sucked in a breath.

"Don't tell me you're shocked." She placed a hand over her heart, attempting to lighten the mood with humor. "You're the one who told me you wanted a temporary arrangement. Alix is doing great now. You should be proud."

"So should you."

She shook her head. "All she ever needed was you. I was just your safety net. You thought she needed me and that helped you get through the tough times. But you did it on your own." Her hand covered his and she tried to memorize its feel and texture. "You did your brother proud, too."

Chelsie swallowed a convulsive sob, determined to get through this without a scene. She'd have plenty of time on the plane and in Florida to cry her heart out. "We agreed to agree when to end this arrangement. I think the time has come. I'll make arrangements with Mrs. Baxter to see Alix during the day while you're up here."

Pain lurked in his eyes, but Chelsie couldn't help him. He'd have to find his way on his own.

"We're partners," he said.

"I think I mentioned what a stupid thing it is to mix business and pleasure, didn't I?" she asked with a fake smile.

His eyes clouded over and Chelsie knew that he, too, was recalling their times together, good and bad. She'd spent the week getting used to the idea, assuring herself that parting company was the only solution. Though Griff could add her to the list of women in his life who had abandoned him, she had the distinction of being the only one who hadn't done so willingly. He wouldn't let her in.

"Pleasure, huh?" he finally asked.

"Oh, yeah. But you were there, so you must remember."

If only he could forget. So why couldn't he let the good times be enough?

She glanced at her watch. "It's time."

Griff knew she meant more than just catching a plane.

"We'll sort out the details when I get back, okay?"

He nodded, at a loss for words. How did you sort out two lives that had become one?

"Before I go, I'll teach you how to make coffee. You need that cup of decaf in the morning. You'll never survive on that mud your secretary makes. Left alone, you'll overdose on caffeine."

He brushed a strand of hair off her cheek. At least she hadn't pulled back this time. "Thanks for caring."

"You know I do." She rose from her seat. "No, maybe you don't," she murmured, shaking her head.

He let her statement pass.

"Have a good flight." And a good life.

"Thanks." Her voice was a mere whisper.

" 'Bye."

She leaned over to kiss him on the cheek. Knowing he was taking unfair advantage, he turned his face at the last moment, so her lips met his. She sucked in a surprise breath before her lips parted, taking him inside. He drank in the taste of her, knowing that he'd never have her again.

When she lifted her head, tears shimmered in her eyes.

A car horn honked. She flashed him a brief smile, one he couldn't return. She turned and walked out.

He stood at the window and watched her get into the waiting cab. She'd be back in three days and out of his life on the fourth. He had only himself to blame. Somehow, the knowledge made things worse.

The phone rang during Sunday morning's breakfast. Griff dove for the receiver, lifting it on the first ring. "Chelsie?"

"Wrong answer."

"Ryan. I'll talk when you get here." In no mood to deal with his friend, Griff hung up. Three days had passed in which he hadn't heard from Chelsie. He hadn't expected to, but he had hoped. Considering he didn't know what he'd say to her should she decide to call, he ought to be grateful for her distance. He wasn't.

He sat back down at the table.

"Pancakes?" Mrs. Baxter asked.

With a shake of his head, he declined. "Just coffee. After this endless weekend, I could use some."

The older woman smiled and handed him a cup. "Decaf." Her eyes twinkled with delight. "Miss Russell said to make sure you stayed away from the hard stuff."

If she didn't intend to stick around, why the hell did Miss Russell care what he drank? Rationally, he realized his anger at Chelsie made little sense. He'd driven her away and caused her to break up the partnership. This morning, however, he wasn't feeling particularly rational.

Alix was in a rotten mood. The little girl whined, cried, and acted out in every way imaginable. She hadn't stopped asking for Chelsie. For Mommy, he silently amended. The word had been on the child's lips morning, noon, and night. And Griff knew without question that this time she wasn't referring to Shannon. Alix wanted Chelsie. And she wasn't the only one. After an entire weekend without a break, Griff's nerves were shot. He needed some peace and quiet.

"Milk," Alix said, pointing to a plastic cup on the counter. He handed her the cup, which Alix immediately knocked over. Milk spilled over the high chair onto the floor and splattered on his jeans and shirt. Frustrated, he opened his mouth to yell, but Alix beat him to it, screaming at the top of her lungs.

"I'll handle it. Go for a walk. Take a break or something," Mrs. Baxter said. "You haven't let me earn my keep the entire weekend. Whatever you're running from, it's bound to catch up with you sometime. Why not deal with it now?"

Griff left the room without a word. Now his housekeeper was offering unsolicited advice. What next?

Ryan caught up with him on the driveway. "Excuse me for stating the obvious, but you look like hell."

"Thanks, Ryan. It's always a pleasure. How'd you get here so fast?"

He patted his jacket pocket. "Cellular. Squirt's been tough?"

"Life's been tougher."

"And I'm sorry for my part in it."

Griff shrugged.

Ryan leaned against the car and squinted against the bright rays of the sun. "You're one pathetic bastard, you know that?"

"Yeah. But you know what they say. It takes one to know one."

"True." He straightened, leaning toward Griff. "What's that on your shirt?"

"Milk," Griff answered without glancing down. The wet spots had already seeped through to his skin. He'd have to change before the odor of dried milk became offensive.

Ryan nodded. "What do you think Deidre would do if she saw you looking like this?"

"I think she'd take the first cab—make that limo—back to her ritzy apartment and shower, just in case the smell interfered with her perfume." Despite himself, Griff couldn't suppress a grin and a full-blown laugh.

"I guess it's a good thing she dumped you."

For the first time, Griff agreed. "True."

"So I guess the next woman's got to love kids."

His laughter suffered a sudden death. "Cut the pop psychology." Telling Ryan about his breakup with Chelsie had been a mistake. After a few beers, Griff had let Ryan pump him for information, forgetting that he'd regret his revelations the next day.

"What the hell is it with you? The first one doesn't like kids and the second one loves 'em. Neither can win."

"Don't compare Chelsie to Deidre," Griff said, taking offense at how his friend had lumped Chelsie with the most selfish woman he'd met. Next to his mother, of course.

Ryan shrugged. "Why the hell not? You have." Ryan started towards the house, stopping to add, "I'm going to visit with my favorite squirt. I'll see you when you're feeling human again."

"Watch her temper. It's lethal."

"Takes after her uncle," he called over his shoulder.

Griff hefted himself up onto the hood of his car. The weather was rapidly changing. Fall would turn to winter. Griff would go back to being a solo practitioner. Cold and lonely. He wondered if he was referring to the season or to himself.

A light breeze blew cold air through his cotton shirt. His skin felt chilled, especially where the milk had settled. A few months ago, he would have been riding in his convertible, top down and probably heading to work, even on Sunday. He'd have been wearing at least a sport jacket, if not a suit and tie. One thing for sure, milk stains wouldn't be anywhere near his designer clothing.

When had he stopped missing his old lifestyle? The days of living for money and the luxuries it brought no longer appealed to him, and he knew for certain it wouldn't have appealed to Chelsie. Time with her had taught him that she was like her sister. Neither valued things above people. Shannon had left her parents' wealthy lifestyle behind to marry his brother.

Chelsie, too, had chosen her own way, just as he had. After his brother's death, Griff had automatically assumed the role of guardian without thought to how his life would change. But it had.

Some changes he'd always regret. The absence of his brother and sister-in-law, for one. Though the pain hadn't subsided completely, he was learning to live with the loss. Hopefully, as he dealt with his grief, he would teach Alix how to live with hers.

Just as Chelsie had done. He couldn't fault her for attempting to bridge the gap with her parents. She had little enough family in her life.

He pressed a hand to his temple and thought of their common bond. Of Alix. Griff had lost his brother, but gained a daughter. He really didn't consider Alix anything less. How could he regret the little girl who had changed his life? She made him more human. She made him have fun. She made him capable of love.

Alix was a part of him. And so was Chelsie.

Griff could no longer remember the man he was before Alix entered his life on a permanent basis. Chelsie had known that other man only by reputation—the one who lived for his work, who didn't care much about anyone or anything other than having fun and making money.

She'd been a part of his transformation. They'd practically raised the little girl together these last few months. If his own life and feelings were forever intertwined with his niece, why did he expect Chelsie to feel different?

She said she loved Alix, and not just as the little girl's aunt. She also said she loved him. How could she separate the two? Love one and not the other? The answer was simple. She couldn't.

Chelsie had accused him of running scared. That much had been true. He had been afraid she'd abandon him. Then, when she pledged her love and promised to stay, he questioned the depth of her feelings. If he continued to lump her in the category of Deidre and his mother, he would always have an excuse to push her away. The old Griff would have done that. The man Alix had taught how to open his heart would not.

So which Griffin Stuart would control his future? The answer was just a start. He had joined the list of men in Chelsie's life to shatter her trust and let her down. Would she believe anything he had to say?

Even if she accepted his words, after watching the scene with her ex-husband, Griff had his doubts about whether she'd put the past behind her completely. She still had one more hurdle to face, though he doubted she was aware of it yet. Considering he had done all the taking so far—her help with Alix, the partnership and the clients she brought in—he could offer this one thing in return. More than an apology was necessary to make Chelsie believe in him. He only hoped he didn't destroy their future in the process.

Heat and humidity hit her as she exited the West Palm Beach airport. Chelsie turned her face toward the sun, grabbing a minute's reprieve before climbing into her rental car and heading for her parents home. She began her drive with fists clenched tight around the steering wheel, her tension mounting with each passing mile.

They expected her arrival, but she had no idea what to expect from them. Having gone most of her childhood without strong support on the home front, she knew she didn't need anything from them in order to survive. But her self-imposed exile, combined with her sister's death, had taken its toll. She might not need anything, but she *wanted* more than she'd received so far.

With Griff all but out of her life in the ways that mattered most, her heart was fragile, her nerves near to breaking. She desperately needed the warmth and understanding only loving parents could provide. Hers had rarely come through. She was here to change things between them before it was too late.

Life's lessons had been hard won for Chelsie. Family was important. She had let hers disintegrate, but she wanted to pick up the pieces. Once she and Griff officially dissolved their partnership, her time with her niece would be more limited than before. She had to make it count. She couldn't offer Alix much, but she could give the child the benefit of relatives who cared and the warmth of family. Mending the ties that remained was also the one thing she could do for herself.

When her parents' exit came up on the turnpike, Chelsie was surprised. She'd passed half an hour lost in thought. She turned into the gated community, slowing as she approached the guardhouse on the left.

"Name?" an older man dressed in white asked.

"Russell."

He checked his clipboard, then raised the electronic gate and waved her through. She was expected, but was she wanted?

She drove down the tree-lined peripheral road that circled the golf course and adjoining homes. Her parents' new sedan sat parked in their driveway. Chelsie's stomach rolled in nervous reaction, re-

minding her of the day she'd tried her first case.
She hoped this experience would turn out better.

She grabbed her bag and stood by the car, glancing at the large, patio-styled home her parents had
purchased last year.

"Chelsie?"

She turned at the sound of her mother's high-
pitched voice, in time to see the older woman step
outside. She hadn't seen Ellen Russell since the day
of the hearing and was surprised to see her well-
groomed mother in walking shorts and an oversized
shirt, looking . . . human. She couldn't help but
wonder if grief had done what nothing else could.

Chelsie went toward her, and when her mother's
arms opened wide, her walk turned into a run.

The morning sun streamed through the kitchen
window. Chelsie blinked into the Florida sunlight.
For the first time in years, she felt at peace in her
parents' home. Although they'd put off the harder
discussions last night, one thing had been clear. The
rift between them had closed.

She picked through the basket of assorted rolls
on the kitchen table and settled herself into a wicker
chair. She popped a piece of blueberry muffin into
her mouth and wondered when the last time was
she'd taken the time to sit down to breakfast, to relax and stop running to work, to meetings, to appointments, to Alix . . . and from life. Setting things
in order now not only felt good, it felt right.

She only wished she hadn't had to lose Griff in
order to reclaim the rest of her life. With one daughter gone, her parents had obviously taken stock. If
they remained understanding and not judgmental,

she'd finally have two loving parents, and Alix would have grandparents who cared and role models to emulate. The mother who'd taken up gardening was far removed from the socialite who had tried to mold both Chelsie and Shannon as they grew up, an emotionally contrite woman who wasn't the same person who had tried to bribe Griff a few months earlier.

The whoosh of the sliding glass door signaled her parents' return from their morning walk. She washed the dry muffin down with a sip of orange juice and turned. "Hi."

"Morning." Her mother, still out of breath, joined her at the table. After grabbing two glasses and pouring juice, so did her father.

"How was your walk?" Chelsie asked.

"Refreshing."

Chelsie laughed. "I'm sorry, but I don't recognize either of you. You two look like a television ad for vitamins or something."

"Instead of one for Tiffany Jewelers?" her mother asked. The older woman didn't join in the laughter.

Time for honesty, Chelsie thought. No matter how hard or what the results. She glanced at her mother. "Well, now that you mention it, yes."

Her mother glanced down at her hands. Skin once soft and smooth now showed signs of work. Chelsie had to admit she was proud of the change. She hoped it extended to her mother's sense of understanding, as well.

"I suppose I deserved that."

Chelsie shook her head and placed her hand on top of her mother's. "No, you didn't. I didn't come here for anger or recriminations."

"Then why did you come?"

"Forgiveness," Chelsie whispered.

"There's nothing to forgive." Her mother's voice cracked.

Her father stepped in to fill the silent void. "We never should have sued Griffin for custody, never should have attempted to bribe him. Never should have used your feelings for your sister as a means to get you to do our dirty work."

"What your father is trying to say is we never blamed you for losing custody. We blamed ourselves for attempting to get it in the first place. That little girl deserves better than we would have given her." Her mother drew a steadying breath. "Better than we gave you and your sister."

Chelsie fought the relief and accompanying dizziness and forced herself to concentrate on their words, words she never thought she'd hear. "Shannon and I had everything growing up." She couldn't bear to hear her parents so full of guilt and blame. They'd lost one daughter and were about to get yet another shock from her.

"Every advantage, yes. I saw to that by working hard and providing you with the upbringing neither your mother nor I had." Darren Russell's low voice was contrite and anguished. Chelsie couldn't remember a time in her life when she'd heard him so honest . . . or so empty.

"We got carried away by the money and the lifestyle," her mother said. "It became more important than people. What people thought of us became more important than our own children or our grandchildren." She glanced down at their intertwined hands. "We were wrong. We lost out on years of more important things, years of closeness with you and your sister, and we're sorry." Her head lowered in shame. "And we'll make it up to you and any grandchildren we're lucky enough to have."

Chelsie swallowed over the painful lump in her throat. They'd given her what she'd always wanted. They'd given her back her parents, while she was about to take away their last dreams. "So am I. And I . . ."

"We don't expect your forgiveness."

She raised damp eyes to meet their expectant gaze. "But you have it. You always have. But . . ." Chelsie inhaled for courage.

"But what?" Her mother rolled her hand over, capturing Chelsie's and holding on tight. "We've been through the worst. I think it's time we heard all of it. Then we can finally be a family."

Chelsie nodded and turned to her mother. Images of Griff and Alix assailed her. The very people who'd given her back her life. She owed it to them to come all the way back, even if Griff no longer wanted any part of her.

She bit the inside of her cheek before speaking. "You . . . you won't be having any more grandchildren," she said. In the minutes that ensued, Chelsie told her parents the same details she'd shared with Griff, and waited for the same painful end.

To her shock and relief, it never came. Her sister's death had changed her parents—too late for Shannon, but just in time for Chelsie.

"Well, at least this wife will be the last woman he abuses." Her father sat with clenched fists, his skin pale beneath the Florida tan.

Chelsie gnawed on the inside of her cheek. "I've

been thinking about that. The system never works quite the way it should. The courts are overcrowded, and given Jeff's propensity to charm and talk his way out of things, he might get off with a hefty fine and community service."

"The man needs help," her father muttered.

"Exactly. And I think I know a way to see he gets it." For Chelsie, it was also a way to make amends for not acting in the past.

Even Griff couldn't fault this idea, considering he, too, wanted assurance that her ex-husband would get the help he needed. Unfortunately, Griff would fight her involvement out of concern. He might not want her in his life, but she knew him well enough to know he'd protect her anyway. Which was why she had no intention of mentioning this particular idea until it was complete.

Her father leaned forward. "I'm listening."

She smiled. He was. After a lifetime of drought, she had unconditional support at last.

Hours later, she knew she'd done the right thing and she'd explain that to her ex-partner when she got home. Since her father had excused himself, Chelsie now sat alone with her mother. She eased back in the family-room recliner.

"Remember, if he doesn't want you, it's his loss." Her mother crossed the room and knelt down beside her.

Despite the painful words, Chelsie burst out laughing.

"What's so funny?" Ellen Russell asked.

"You're talking to me like I'm a teenager and I've lost my first true love."

Her mother reached out and touched her hair. "Haven't you?"

"Haven't I what?" Chelsie asked. She'd been brutally honest about everything in her life except her relationship with Griff. That particular loss was still too painful and fresh.

Her mother's wise gaze met hers. "Lost your first true love?"

Chelsie opened and closed her mouth, unable to form an answer. Apparently a mother never lost her intuition, even after years of neglect.

"I lost your teenage years in a selfish fog, but I'm here now. And I know what I see."

"What's that?" Chelsie asked, too emotionally spent to get her anger up or argue.

"A heartbroken woman. And I know as sure as we're sitting in this room, talking like mother and daughter, that your pain has nothing to do with your ex-husband and everything to do with Griff."

She blinked back tears, but they fell anyway. Then Chelsie did the one thing she needed most. She cried in her mother's arms.

The roar of airplanes sounded in the distance as Chelsie bid good-bye to her parents at the airport.

"We'll be back at the end of the month," her father promised, "apology in hand and knocking on that man's door to see our granddaughter."

Her father had referred to Griff as *that man* ever since her mother had informed him he'd turned Chelsie away. In her opinion, they were taking the parent routine too far, but they'd get past it. "I'm sure I can arrange visits. He's not unreasonable,

Dad. And given everything you put him through, an apology would help ease things between you."

"I'll do it, but after what he did to you . . ."

"That's between us, and you owe him." She leaned over and kissed her father's weathered cheek.

"I know. But I still don't like what went on between you two."

"Like you said, Dad, it went on between us. Stay out of it."

He turned towards his wife. "I'm good enough to talk to when it comes to dealing with her son-of-a-bitch ex-husband, but when it comes to . . ."

"The man she loves, it's none of your business."

Chelsie looked at her parents and laughed. Two people who had learned life's lessons the harshest possible way, but still remained together. She wished Griff could see them now. Maybe he'd believe anything was possible.

She thought of his past and his pain and knew she was wishing for the impossible.

THIRTEEN

Griff turned onto the busy street. The modern office building he sought appeared on his left.

"Last chance to back out." Ryan thumped his hand against the dashboard of the car.

The time had long passed to second-guess his decision. So much of his life and his future rode on this meeting. Griff turned the steering wheel, angling the car into the nearest parking spot in the underground lot. "No way in hell. You?" He glanced at Ryan.

"Nope."

Griff had known the answer before he asked the question. Ryan had never deserted him in the past. He wouldn't start now. The trust he placed in his friend had taught him a valuable lesson, one he intended to extend to Chelsie. Both people were loyal and cared for him. Griff only wished he'd heeded what was in front of him for so long.

They walked through the dark lot and into the building. A security guard greeted them at the front entrance. "Stevens and McLaughlin," Griff said. "We have an appointment with one of the attorneys."

The burly man in the gray suit nodded. "Sign in."

Griff scrawled his name. Ryan did the same. "Fifth floor," the guard said.

They stepped into the elevators. "So far, so good." Griff rolled his shoulders. "Take it easy, Ryan. The hard part's yet to come." Griff had no illusions about dealing with the man Chelsie had once called her husband. He hadn't reached the top of his profession by letting other people have their way easily.

"I can handle it."

"We'll see. Just stand behind me and keep your mouth shut."

Ryan frowned. "Yeah. I never should have agreed."

"But you did." His friend wouldn't be here otherwise. Griff would have liked to handle Jeff Sutton on his own, but Ryan's persistence couldn't be ignored. Besides, the backup would shore up his points with Chelsie's ex and ensure the outcome. Two men would intimidate Sutton much more than one, but Ryan's temper tended to get in the way of common sense.

Griff needed cool heads and clear thinking for his plan to work. He was counting on the self-serving side of Jeff Sutton's personality to swing things their way. He could at least give Chelsie back her life before truly placing his trust in her hands.

The receptionist took one look at Griff in his three-piece suit and Ryan in his favorite jeans and leather jacket and led them back to Jeff Sutton's office without argument.

The young woman raised her hand to knock on the office door. "We can take it from here," Ryan said.

"He prefers to be notified when he has unexpected company," she said.

"Then we wouldn't be unexpected, would we?" Griff asked. "It's okay. We're old friends."

The woman looked uncertain.

"I'll say you were indisposed and we walked ourselves in." Ryan gave her a wink that had been charming women throughout the years.

She blushed, looking flustered. "Go ahead." They waited until the receptionist disappeared down the hall and around the corner.

"After you," Ryan said with a grin. "I'll just hold up the wall and keep my mouth shut. For as long as I can stand it," he muttered under his breath.

Griff rapped once with his knuckles. Without waiting for a reply, he walked inside. Jeff Sutton sat behind a large wooden desk, looking every inch the self-important attorney.

"What the hell?" His gaze shifted from the documents in his hand to his visitors. He pushed himself to his feet. "Who let you in?"

Griff stepped inside. Ryan followed and slammed the door shut behind him. "Consider this a pre-trial hearing," Griff said.

Sutton reached for the phone. Ryan swerved behind Griff and slammed his hand down on the receiver.

So much for holding up the wall, Griff thought. "I hear you like deals, so I've got one for you," he said to Chelsie's ex. Reaching beneath his jacket to the inside pocket, he withdrew a small manila envelope.

Chelsie's ex-husband paled at the sight. "I'm listening."

"You're a smart man." Griff opened the envelope

and began laying out pictures, face up on the desk. Some photos were of Amanda, others of Chelsie. None were pretty. "I call this evidence. I have copies, by the way. You're a partner." Griff glanced around the man's office. "Nice digs. I assume you want to keep them as well as your clients and your *good name.*"

Ryan coughed in blatant disgust.

Griff ignored him, concentrating on Jeff Sutton. "Here are the terms. Fly to the Caribbean and obtain a quick divorce, agree to twice-weekly counseling, and stay the hell away from your ex-wives and women in general until you get your act together. You don't, and these go public."

Sutton flicked the photos with his one free hand. "Blackmail. I don't have to take this crap from you."

Griff shook his head. "Look, buddy do you want to go to trial and make things public?" He shrugged. "My pleasure. I'm just giving you an option we can all live with. I can't get disbarred for offering you a settlement. You, on the other hand, can do jail time if you don't accept. I can live with either option."

Which wasn't exactly true. Griff had done his homework. The family courts were clogged with cases like these. Statistically, a man like Jeff Sutton would be slapped with a continued restraining order at best, and maybe some court-ordered counseling, nothing as intense as what Griff and Ryan had in mind. Keeping him away from Chelsie and Amanda was of paramount importance. Preventing him from harming other women was also a consideration.

"By the way," Ryan said, removing his hand from atop Sutton's. "Did I mention I'm a private investigator? I'm an expert at tailing people. I'll know your every move, buddy. One missed counseling session and you're ours." He punched his hand into his other palm for emphasis.

Griff stifled a groan. Ryan had often gone overboard, even as a kid. The threat to this man's career would have been enough to keep him toeing the line. It was all that truly mattered to him in his pathetic life.

Sutton glared at Ryan and shook his hand out as if he'd been injured. The man didn't even understand the irony. Griff would like to kick his teeth down his throat for what he'd done to Chelsie, but refrained. He was taking the best route for everyone involved.

"Well?" Griff asked.

"What about my son?"

About time the man got around to what was truly important in life, Griff thought. He shrugged. "For now, you sign away custody. A few years from now, if the psychiatrist tells me you're a fit human being, we'll consider renegotiating the deal."

"This is extortion," he yelled.

Griff shook his head. "It's a fair offer. You like this corner office and your so-called reputation. I suggest you accept. The papers will be here by four this afternoon. Sign them by tomorrow." He gathered the pictures together in his hand.

The other man's face flushed an angry shade of red. "Just like a woman to send you two to do her dirty work," Sutton muttered. "Chelsie should have taken me at my word."

"Excuse me?" If Chelsie had been in contact with her ex-husband, this was the first Griff had heard about it. If it was true, he'd throttle her himself. His stomach churned at the very notion. At least she had the eastern seaboard separating her from her violent past, he thought. But the protective feeling he'd begun to accept as normal when it came to Chelsie remained with him.

Sutton sat back in his seat, hopefully beginning to accept defeat. "She called the other day to broker this same deal."

"You figured you could weasel your way out."

"I don't answer to her. Besides, she didn't mention surveillance or you and your bouncer buddy here." He gestured to Ryan.

Griff bent down over the desk, making sure he towered over the man who had no compulsion about hurting women, but who cowered before men his own size. "Listen well. You so much as breathe in her direction, you answer to me." Griff made a show of lining the pictures up and placing them back in his pocket.

The thought of Chelsie having anything to do with this slime, even long distance, made his skin crawl. Yet he admired her courage and the foresight it took for her to come up with the same plan he and Ryan had formulated together.

"Let me ask you a question, Sutton."

The man raised defeated eyes to his.

"Doesn't it even bother you, what you did to those two women?" The two they knew about, Griff silently added. He didn't want to think there could be others and hoped this deal would prevent further victims.

"They asked for it. It's not my fault they push a guy to the end of his rope. I never meant to hurt either of them."

Figures. Griff shook his head. He just wanted Jeff

out of their lives and less of a threat to womenkind. "Then do yourself a favor. Take this deal and get yourself some help."

Without a second glance, Griff turned and walked out. Ryan followed. The easy part was behind him. The hard part was yet to come. Chelsie returned today, and Griff's life hung in the balance.

"How was your trip?" Griff looked at his partner with hungry eyes after a weekend of deprivation.

Chelsie wore jeans, an old sweatshirt, and a ponytail with stray strands of hair falling around her neck. Not a woman dressed for work, that much he knew. She obviously hadn't changed her mind about severing their partnership. Nor could he ask her to.

His stomach churned with dread, but he remained calm. His perspective may have changed, but she didn't know it, and he'd put her through hell. She deserved to make her own decisions about her future.

"Not bad if you like heat and humidity," she said.

"Did you get much sun?"

She laughed, but it sounded strained. "Not all that much."

"Could we move past the weather?" Otherwise they'd become exactly what he feared most. Friendly adversaries, two people who cared too much, but couldn't get past their opposing points of view. He couldn't live with that. In fact, he flat out refused to try.

She looked startled at his unnecessarily abrupt tone, then shrugged. "Okay. The trip was productive."

"They've forgiven you?"

"Actually, they never blamed me as much as they blamed themselves. But my parents were never the warm type and they didn't know how to show what they were feeling."

"So they retreated to Florida to lick their wounds?"

She tilted her head, obviously assessing his sincerity. "To heal, Griff. To get over losing a daughter, to come to terms with the kind of people they'd become."

"I know that." Just watching the play of emotions over her face, listening to her defense of people she didn't understand but still loved, how could he not?

"I can't justify their attempt to bribe you, but they realize they were wrong. And now that they've begun to readjust their priorities and are trying to live without Shannon, they'll come back home soon."

She glanced up, meeting his gaze with serious, imploring eyes. "They miss Alix. They'd like to see her, and I'd like them to be her family, if you'll let them."

How like Chelsie to put her parents' needs before her own, to risk his anger by pressing their case. "Of course they can see her. I never said they couldn't."

As Chelsie's parents and Alix's grandparents, he'd have to make peace with them eventually. It helped that they'd won Chelsie over, but it wasn't a necessity. Blood bound them to his niece. He'd have given them another chance regardless. He paused before asking, "Did you tell them about your past?"

She nodded. "It was hard, but necessary—and in the end, cleansing for me. Very shocking for them. But the truth is out in the open now." Her warm, dark eyes met his. "For all of us."

"Speaking of truths, when were you going to tell me you'd been in touch with your ex?"

Her eyes narrowed. "At the same time you told me you'd done the same," she said, challenge lacing her words.

Griff couldn't help it. He burst out laughing. "I should have known you'd be one step ahead of me."

"I've been in contact with Amanda. You shouldn't have done it, Griff."

"Neither should you. Why don't we call it a good business decision and leave it at that?"

A smile tugged at the edges of her mouth. "It was a good plan."

"Had to be. We both came up with it."

"Yeah, we did." She laughed again, and the heaviness weighting down his heart this last weekend seemed to ease.

From the side of her desk, she lifted an empty carton and placed it on top. His stomach twisted again. Once she made a decision, Chelsie obviously didn't waste any time implementing it.

Forcing normal conversation while she packed to desert him wasn't easy, but he managed. "How did your parents take the news?" he asked of her parents' reaction to her abusive marriage.

"They didn't fault me for any of my decisions."

"That's because you weren't to blame."

She smiled. "Thanks. It took me five long years to realize that, but at least it's behind me now." While she spoke, she transferred her books, tape dispenser, and other belongings from her desk into the large carton. When she reached for the tiny silver frames, he knew he was in trouble.

But because the distraction kept her talking without any awkward silences, Griff let her continue. Her weekend had been as cathartic as his. He wanted to hear as much as she was willing to divulge.

"Guess what?" she asked.

The pleased tone in her voice made him wary. "What?"

"I sublet my apartment, furniture and all." Turning away, she began to collect books from the shelf behind the desk. "Before I left, I put up a sign. Someone left a message while I was away. Two law students love the area and were waiting for an opening in my building."

"When do they want to move in?"

"The end of the month," she said.

Two weeks away. "What made you decide to do that?"

She turned away from the bookshelves and she looked at him. "I don't need it anymore."

"I don't understand."

"It's simple. I realized exactly why I'd chosen that apartment and decorated it the way I had—for the same reasons I pulled away from my sister and never allowed myself to get too close to Alix. All that crystal and glass told me every day that there would never be a child in my life."

"And then I pulled you into our lives."

"I think I pushed first," she said, but she nodded, then squeezed her arms tight across her chest.

Griff knew the next few minutes were going to be painful for them both. He also knew that they were necessary if they wanted a future. And that was the problem. Although he now knew what he wanted, her thoughts and feelings were by no means transparent.

She'd closed herself off from him and he wanted back in. He'd thought this had to be accomplished in stages. Business first, personal later. He hadn't liked it, but he'd understood. Having Chelsie in his future was well worth the wait. If she was planning on moving, he had less time than he originally thought.

"I did a lot of thinking this weekend about what you said before I left," she said.

Apparently he was about to get his wish. "I said a lot of things." None particularly correct or rational, he thought, preparing himself for the verbal blast that was to come.

"Well, you were right about this one. I did love the idea of what you could give me. I loved the notion of a child and a husband who loved me, of a family that would be there every day when I got home. I wanted what I had growing up, but more. More emotion, more family." She brushed at the stray tears dripping down her face, then wiped her wet hands on her jeans.

He wanted to spare her, to tell her that none of this mattered, but he could see in her eyes that it did.

"You wanted me to separate my feelings. I did that. I told you I loved you apart from my feelings for my niece. But that wasn't enough. You wanted proof that I wasn't using you and I can't give you that. How can I?" She swallowed, choking on her words and her emotions.

He grasped her arms, noticing that her entire body trembled beneath his touch. "None of that matters."

"I know. Because I realized something else this weekend."

"What?"

"Even if you took that leap and believed in my feelings, it wouldn't work. You'd end up resenting me in the end because I couldn't give you your own child."

Shifting positions, he wrapped one arm around her shoulders and led her to the couch. "Sit."

She complied and he settled himself next to her. "I asked you before. Where did you get such nonsense?"

"From you." She ran her tanned fingers over the raised pattern in the sofa, refusing to meet his gaze. "You love kids. You told me you'd like another."

"Another doesn't necessarily mean one of my own."

She shrugged, as if dismissing his words as meaningless, although they were probably the most important he'd ever spoken. She just wasn't hearing him, proof that his plan of winning her over in stages was necessary.

Although she claimed to want a family, she wasn't ready. She would never believe he'd changed his mind, not without time and concrete proof.

"You and Jared had a rough life, but you bought this house. It's got a bunch of empty rooms. I've seen you with Alix." She jumped up from her seat. "Why are we even discussing this? You made things clear before I left."

"Yes, I guess I did."

She bit down on her lip and nodded. "Okay, then. Boxes await."

"Not yet."

"Why draw out the inevitable?" she asked.

"Because maybe it isn't. What's the one thing your clients expect of you?"

She stared at him. "What's going on, Griff?"

Apparently she wasn't about to let him ease into this. "I want to keep our partnership alive." In more ways than one, he thought.

"Impossible."

"No. Dissolving it is. Your clients expect stability and an attorney they can trust. Not one who changes partners on a whim, gets involved, then backs off. You said yourself these women have fragile psyches. They need what *we* can offer them. If you back out now, you'll scare them. They'll think they can't trust you to be there for the long haul. Is that what you want?"

She glared at him. "You don't play fair, Griff."

"Maybe not, but I play honest. And, sweetheart, this is as honest as it gets. So do I still have a partner, partner?" He extended his hand towards her.

"It's not like you've given me a choice," she muttered.

He groaned aloud. He wanted her by his side, but he wanted her to be there because she believed in him, believed they could have a future. No more stalling, he thought. "Come with me."

Her eyes narrowed. "Where?"

Grasping her hand, he gave a gentle pull. Chelsie followed reluctantly. She wanted to get this morning over with as soon as possible. Her trip to Florida and the reconciliation with her parents had helped her put life in some sort of perspective and she'd reached a crossroads. It was time to move forward. She'd survive without Griff. After all, she'd lived through worse. But not much, she thought, glancing at the man she loved.

Chelsie found herself in the downstairs den. Mrs. Baxter was attempting to fold laundry, while Alix thwarted her at every turn. No sooner would Mrs. Baxter fold an item than Alix would toss it in the air, undoing the older woman's work.

Griff cleared his throat.

Alix glanced up from her important task. When her eyes lit on Chelsie, she let out an excited squeal and flew across the room.

Chelsie knelt down to catch her and fell backwards beneath the child's assault. She laughed aloud. This little girl's happiness was worth everything.

With much effort, Chelsie managed to maneuver into a sitting position and bring the little girl into her lap. From the corner of her eye, she saw Mrs. Baxter collect the scattered clothing and leave the room, laundry basket in hand.

Grateful for Alix's warm welcome, Chelsie buried her head in the little girl's neck, tickling her tummy at the same time. Her hair smelled of baby shampoo and talcum powder. A lump formed in Chelsie's throat.

Griff's insistence on keeping their partnership alive was based on valid business points, but he'd also given her a personal reprieve. Although things would never go back to the way they'd once been, the family dinners and the shared laughter, at least she'd be closer to Alix than she'd originally thought. The little girl twined her chubby fingers into Chelsie's hair.

Chelsie laughed, then glanced over Alix's head at

Griff. He watched her with a strange expression on his face. "Well?" he asked.

"I guess she missed me, too."

"Are you saying you missed her?"

"You know I did." She inhaled, drawing on her stored energy. She'd be working in this house, but she wouldn't be playing mommy anymore. The thought hurt. "That's why we also need to work out scheduled times for me to see her, so she has some regularity in her life."

She closed her eyes, realizing that she'd just given Griff more proof that her niece was a priority in her life. She was beginning to understand why he would never believe she loved him unconditionally and apart from his guardianship of Alix.

"Maybe."

Her eyes opened wide. She'd never really expected him to deny her request, but she'd fight him if he did.

"After we settle one thing."

Alix jumped off her lap and walked over to the cocktail table, pulling a thick magazine onto the floor. She contented herself ripping pages out of the center one at a time. Chelsie wanted to laugh, but she couldn't focus on anything but Griff's words.

"Settle what?"

He leaned against the wall. He'd pushed the sleeves of his navy sweater around his forearms and stuffed his hands into the front pocket of his khaki pants. "How much do you love her?"

"Is this a trick question?" Too much and she would prove Griff's accusation correct. Too little and he'd begrudge her time with Alix.

"No. Just give me an honest answer."

She nodded, deciding to tell him the truth. Except for liberal visiting privileges, she had nothing left to lose. "As much as if she were my own daughter, if not more."

"Me, too." He smiled, an open, honest smile that was so devastating in its impact that Chelsie almost forgot to breathe.

He cupped her face in his hands. "I love you. And I *was* looking for excuses to drive you away. But not anymore."

"No?" She gazed at him through narrowed eyes. Never in her life had Chelsie wanted to believe in anyone or anything as badly as she wanted to believe Griff, but the hurt he'd inflicted still ran deep.

"Never again." He brushed her lips with his, then rested his forehead against hers. "I barely remember who I was before I met you. I'd already been lost when Jared died. Afterwards, I went through the motions of living for Alix's sake. But she wasn't doing so hot, either, so we turned to you. And you saved us both."

She shook her head in denial.

"Yes. We all started to live again. Even you. You'd buried yourself in that damned apartment and made sure you had enough work to cover every hour of every day. You didn't have to remember and you didn't have to feel." He lifted his head and looked in her eyes. "Just like me."

She opened her mouth to speak, but the words lodged in her throat. He was giving her everything she wanted, but she still couldn't believe he'd changed his mind overnight. More importantly, she still couldn't give him the children he both wanted and deserved. "What are you saying?" she asked.

"That I love you. I know I've given you every reason not to trust me or what I say, but that's past. And I plan to prove it."

"Griff, I . . ."

He placed a warm finger over her lips. "Not another word. I wanted you to hear the words. Believing them will come."

How had he known what she was thinking? Her heart pounded painfully in her chest. She'd learned what was important in life. Love, family, and trust were the things that counted most. She and Griff had the first two, but something important was missing. He hadn't trusted her at the moment she'd needed him most.

How could she know for sure he wouldn't rip away her security once again? How could she know he wouldn't come to resent her for not being able to give him the family he said he wanted?

Griff studied her intently, those dark eyes imploring her to believe.

He'd secured their partnership despite her belief that it was over. She wondered if he could do the same for the rest of their lives.

Chelsie stood by the copy machine, waiting as it spewed out pages of a deposition transcript. With Griff in court this afternoon, the office was quiet. No hum of his low voice on the telephone, no incessant questions about family law and basic interviewing technique—questions he could have figured out for himself at this point, since Amanda had spread word of Griff and Chelsie's practice throughout the women's shelter. In just one short week, he carried his share of their workload and handled each case in a unique manner appropriate to the individual client. He was doing well and didn't need her opinion on every minute detail, yet he asked anyway.

An excuse to be near her. She'd recognized his ploy for what it was, had even called him on it once. He'd merely laughed and reminded her dinner was at six. No excuses allowed.

That was another thing. Laughter came freer and more often around here now, for them both. She caught herself smiling at the thought. Was this what was called building trust? If so, she liked it.

The office doorbell rang. She glanced at her watch. Four-thirty, last delivery for the day. If the package contained the documents she thought, she'd be up for the better part of the night preparing for a deposition tomorrow. If not, she'd be asking for a delay.

She opened the door.

"For you," the delivery man said.

"Thanks, Frank."

"Sign here. This one's your signature only."

She raised an eyebrow and did as he asked.

"Have a good one." He turned and headed back down the path.

Curious, she tore open the seal, pulled out the official documents inside, and began to read. Custody papers. Legal, valid change-of-custody papers for the minor child Alix Stuart.

Chelsie's heart slammed in rapid rhythm against her rib cage. She'd wondered if Griff could possibly cement their future by convincing her he believed she loved him separate and apart from her feelings for her sister's child. She'd wondered if he'd change his mind about not wanting children of his own.

And now she knew.

"I'm telling you, women aren't worth the effort," Ryan muttered. He grabbed a can of cola from the refrigerator and sank into the nearest kitchen chair.

"Big change in tune. Guess your latest girlfriend dumped you," Griff said with a laugh.

Ryan shrugged. "She couldn't stand the hours." He took a swig of his drink and kicked his feet out in front of him.

Following his friend's cue, Griff loosened the knot on his constricting tie. "Ever think of settling down?" Griff asked.

Ryan raised his eyebrows. "Find me what you've got and maybe I'll consider it."

"Tell me what I've got and I'll try and help you out." Since her return from Florida, Griff had had one hell of a time figuring out where he stood with Chelsie.

"Pathetic. Both of us," Ryan said and finished the soda in one large gulp.

Griff agreed. He also wondered if it was about to get worse. Knowing she needed some normalcy, Griff had bided his time before pulling out the last weapon in his arsenal. It had taken him a week of sleepless nights to figure out the one thing that would cement their lives together at last—at least he hoped so.

If Chelsie wasn't swayed after today, there would be nothing left to say. Hell, he'd sever the partnership himself. He couldn't see her professionally and not have her in his life when the workday ended.

Footsteps sounded on the back stairs leading from the house to the office. He turned to Ryan. "Not that I don't appreciate the ride back from the office, but don't you have some place to be?" He'd left Mrs. Baxter his car so she could do the long-overdue food shopping.

Footsteps were replaced by a loud knocking on the adjoining door. Ryan turned towards the noise. "Don't you think you could give her a key?" he asked. "Might make her feel more welcome."

Griff rolled his eyes. "Tell you what," he said as he walked towards the door. "You make yourself scarce, I'll give Chelsie that key. Then she can lock *you* out."

Ryan rose and tossed the soda can into the recycling bin beneath the cabinet under the sink. "There's loyalty for you. I'm going, but one thing first."

Griff reached for the handle on the door. "What's that?" He opened the door to see Chelsie on the other side.

"Invite me to the wedding," Ryan said as he paused in front of her.

"What wedding is that?" she asked.

Ryan shrugged. "Ask your partner. Good seeing you again, Chels."

"You too, Ryan," she said to his retreating back.

The door closed behind him and Griff got his first good look at Chelsie. Cheeks flushed and eyes bright, she stood before him, waving a piece of paper in her hand. *The* piece of paper.

Griff held his breath.

"What is this?" she asked.

"Come." He reached out and took her hand, leading her into the family room. With both hands on her shoulders, he eased her onto the soft cushions. "What is it you said to me when I proposed you help out with Alix?" he asked her.

She looked at him, puzzled.

He wondered if his heart had ever beat so hard or so fast. He wondered if he'd ever had as much at stake. "Let me remind you. You asked what would happen when I decided Alix was doing well enough to throw you out of her life *again*."

She glanced down at the custody papers in her hands. "I still don't understand what you meant . . . why you . . ."

"I gave you unconditional joint custody. Any schedule you want, any way you want."

"Aren't you afraid I'll take her away from you somehow? You aren't worried that maybe my parents will use this against you to sue for custody again?"

"Your parents. Well, they're the unknown in all this. They're a risk," he admitted. One he'd struggled with long and hard all week.

But he'd accused Chelsie of wanting his ready-made family and then walked away instead of accepting her word, instead of believing she loved him separate and apart from Alix. He'd hurt her so deeply he still saw it in her expression every time they were together.

Her shadowed eyes haunted his dreams. She was the last person he'd ever hurt intentionally. He saw only one way to make amends and hopefully assure their future. The only means he had to convince her of his trust was to offer the one thing he'd accused her of wanting more than him. His niece.

He couldn't think of another way to bring them

together, except to risk everything. He knelt down
and stared into her eyes. "Listen to me. I love you.
I want to marry you and be a real family. But if you
can't see beyond my mistakes, I understand. I'll accept any type of shared custody arrangement you
want. I'll . . ."

She cut him off by throwing her arms around his
neck and toppling them both to the floor. "I take
it this arrangement works for you?" he asked, out
of breath but still needing to hear the words.

"I'm overwhelmed," she said. "You'd do that for
me?"

"Love you? Yes. Marry you? Yes."

"Share custody of Alix even if I said no to your
proposal," Chelsie said softly.

"In a heartbeat." Although right now he was fairly
certain his own heart had stopped.

She blinked against moist eyes. "Can you move?"

"Your point?" he asked. Because if she didn't answer him soon, he might not make it another minute.

"You're not going anywhere, Griff, and neither
am I." Chelsie looked down at the man she loved,
the man who had risked his emotional nightmare
to give her what he believed she needed. What he
failed to realize was the depth of that love. "You
didn't need to do this. I believed you when you said
you trusted me. It's just that I can't give you all you
deserve. The family you want, a child of your
own . . ."

He grasped her cheeks in both hands, forcing her
to look him in the eye. "Your words, Chelsie. *Not
mine.* I said more children. Our children."

She swallowed hard and tried again. "Are you sure?"

"Sure that I love you? Yes. Sure that I want to spend the rest of my life with you? Yes to that, too."

"Sure that you can accept not having children of your own?" She asked because she had to be sure. More importantly, *he* had to be sure.

His eyes never left Chelsie's face. "I already have all that I want. And you're right. I do want more kids." His fingertips brushed at the tear on her cheek. "So why wouldn't I love any child you and I decided to adopt?"

"Adopt?"

"We both love Alix as if she were our own. As long as any other children are ours to raise and love together, why would I want more?"

Her throat hurt from holding back tears. "Are you sure?"

"That again?" he asked with a grin. He pulled her down onto the floor with him until his arms encircled her, squeezing her so tight she couldn't help but be certain. "I'm sure," he whispered. "Are you?"

Beyond words, Chelsie merely nodded. She had all she ever wanted and more than she'd ever dreamed.

"Now that we've got that settled, we can plan ahead."

She lay her head on his shoulder and felt his strength. He'd be there for her always. She laughed. "Okay, let's plan," she agreed.

"For starters, I guess it's a good thing you sublet your apartment after all."

She feigned a loud gasp and propped herself up

to look at the face she adored. "But what about that town house I rented?"

Panic flared in his eyes, causing her to shake her head in laughter and denial. "Gotcha," Chelsie said with a grin, grateful for the love and the laughter she had found.

"That you do," he whispered.

She wrapped her arms around him, thankful she'd been given so much.

"I don't plan on ever letting you go."

She smiled. "Who asked you to?"

"No more doubts? Because from now on we share everything, good and bad."

Chelsie smiled. "I'll share my life with you, Griff. All you had to do was ask."

ABOUT THE AUTHOR

Karen Drogin lives in Purchase, New York, with her husband and two young daughters. A former practicing attorney, Karen is more at home writing romance than legal briefs. She loves to read as much as she loves to write and would enjoy hearing from those who feel the same! Write Karen care of Kensington Books or e-mail at Carlyphil@aol.com. You can check out Karen's Web site at http://www.eclectics.com/carlyphillips.

BOOK YOUR PLACE ON OUR WEBSITE AND MAKE THE READING CONNECTION!

We've created a customized website just for our very special readers, where you can get the inside scoop on everything that's going on with Zebra, Pinnacle and Kensington books.

When you come online, you'll have the exciting opportunity to:

- View covers of upcoming books

- Read sample chapters

- Learn about our future publishing schedule (listed by publication month *and author*)

- Find out when your favorite authors will be visiting a city near you

- Search for and order backlist books from our online catalog

- Check out author bios and background information

- Send e-mail to your favorite authors

- Meet the Kensington staff online

- Join us in weekly chats with authors, readers and other guests

- Get writing guidelines

- AND MUCH MORE!

Visit our website at
http://www.zebrabooks.com